True Riders

MARGUERITE HENRY'S

Ponies *of* Chincoteague

◆ True Riders ◆

CATHERINE HAPKA

Aladdin

New York London Toronto Sydney New Delhi

This book is a work of fiction. Any references to historical events, real people, or
real places are used fictitiously. Other names, characters, places, and events are
products of the author's imagination, and any resemblance to actual events
or places or persons, living or dead, is entirely coincidental.

ALADDIN

An imprint of Simon & Schuster Children's Publishing Division
1230 Avenue of the Americas, New York, NY 10020
This Aladdin paperback edition November 2015
Text copyright © 2015 by The Estate of Marguerite Henry
Cover illustration copyright © 2015 by Robert Papp
Also available in an Aladdin hardcover edition.
All rights reserved, including the right of reproduction in whole or in part in any form.
ALADDIN is a trademark of Simon & Schuster, Inc., and related logo is
a registered trademark of Simon & Schuster, Inc.
For information about special discounts for bulk purchases, please contact
Simon & Schuster Special Sales at 1-866-506-1949 or business@simonandschuster.com.
The Simon & Schuster Speakers Bureau can bring authors to your live event.
For more information or to book an event contact the Simon & Schuster Speakers Bureau
at 1-866-248-3049 or visit our website at www.simonspeakers.com.
Book designed by Karina Granda
The text of this book was set in Adobe Caslon Pro.
Manufactured in the United States of America 1015 OFF
2 4 6 8 10 9 7 5 3 1
Library of Congress Control Number 2015945387
ISBN 978-1-4814-3972-5 (hc)
ISBN 978-1-4814-3971-8 (pbk)
ISBN 978-1-4814-3973-2 (eBook)

True Riders

◆ CHAPTER ◆
1

BROOKE RHODES STARED OUT THE CLASS-
room window, watching as a brightly colored maple leaf
floated lazily to the ground on the breeze. A second later
a gust of wind rattled the panes, sending more autumn
leaves whirling crazily across the school yard.

Stifling a yawn and pushing her glasses up her nose,
Brooke glanced at the clock over the classroom door.
English was her last class of the day, and she couldn't wait
to get out of there. The school was overheated and stuffy,
making her feel sleepy.

Or maybe it was boredom making her feel that way.
At the front of the room, Benji Finnegan was droning

on and on about a plane crash and an axe. The class had been doing oral book reports for the past couple of days—Brooke's report on *The Secret Garden* had been on Friday—and it seemed to be taking forever to get through them all.

Brooke shifted in her chair, willing the hands of the clock to move faster. It was only Monday, but Brooke was already looking forward to the weekend. She hoped she would get to spend it exactly as she'd spent the past weekend—with Foxy.

Just thinking about her spunky Chincoteague pony made Brooke smile. Foxy was still young—only five and a half years old—and still learning about being a riding horse. Brooke had owned the flaxen chestnut mare since she was a yearling and had done most of Foxy's training herself, though she'd had plenty of help and advice from books, websites, and especially her neighbors, who'd owned horses for ages.

And of course, for the past almost-two years, she'd also had lots of advice and encouragement from the Pony Post, a private online message board with just four members, all of them crazy about Chincoteague ponies.

Brooke had never met the other three members in person but still considered them among her very best friends. In fact, she sometimes thought she knew more about them than she did about her real-life friends right there in Maryland.

For instance, she knew that Haley Duncan took her chosen sport of eventing very seriously. She trained and competed as much as she could with her pony, Wings, a lively pinto gelding she free leased from a neighbor. Earlier that fall Haley and Wings had participated in a riding clinic with a world-famous eventer who'd probably be competing in the Olympics someday soon. Brooke had no dreams of Olympic glory herself, but hearing about Haley's experience at the clinic had inspired Brooke to take her own riding and training a little more seriously.

Then there was Nina Peralt. She lived in New Orleans and had recently ridden her pony, Bay Breeze, in a show at her boarding barn. The two of them had done well, but more important, they'd had fun. In fact, Nina seemed to have fun no matter what she was doing, which helped Brooke remember not to take things too seriously.

The final member of the Pony Post was Maddie Martinez, who lived in Northern California. She didn't own a pony herself but rode a Chincoteague mare named Cloudy at her lesson stable. Brooke admired the way Maddie was practically fearless and took everything in stride—which was pretty much the opposite of how Brooke felt most of the time. But she liked to think that just knowing Maddie had made her a little braver.

I was totally channeling all three of them this weekend during my rides, Brooke thought, remembering the way she'd stayed focused, not letting Foxy's prancing scare her out of convincing the mare to do a proper turn on the forehand. And then Brooke had celebrated finally getting it right by going on a nice, relaxing trail ride afterward.

She and Foxy had been having a lot of fun lately. But hearing about what her friends had been doing—Haley's clinic, Nina's show—had made Brooke wonder if she and Foxy should be making even more progress than they were.

Haley and the others are always talking about how much fun jumping is, she thought. *It's getting cold, but the ground isn't frozen yet. Maybe we should try to get back to that part of our training.*

She nodded, liking the idea. Back in the summer her stepfather had surprised her with two weeks at riding camp for her and Foxy. The two of them had learned a lot there, including the basics of jumping. While Brooke had done her best to keep practicing most of the stuff they'd learned, she hadn't done much jumping other than hopping over the occasional log in the woods near her house. While she'd had a makeshift riding ring in the corner of Foxy's pasture for years, she didn't have any real jumps there—just a few beat-up traffic cones her stepfather had brought home from the used car lot, and a couple of fence posts she'd used to make obstacle courses to practice steering.

Maybe I can ask Adam to help me build some real jumps, Brooke thought. *If he has time, that is.*

She sneaked a peek over her shoulder. Adam Conley was sitting in the back row with the Webb twins. All three boys were goofing off, smacking one another and giggling whenever the teacher wasn't looking their way.

Brooke rolled her eyes and turned around again. What did Adam see in those guys, anyway? He'd never hung out with them before this year.

At that moment Benji finally finished his report and sat down. Ms. Neal consulted the chart on her desk. "Kiersten, you're next," she announced. "Go ahead."

Brooke watched as Kiersten Ellis walked to the front of the room clutching a stapled sheaf of papers. Kiersten was new. She'd joined their class just a couple of weeks earlier. She was a little taller than Brooke and just as slender, with glossy dark brown hair that reached almost to her waist. She was wearing boots that looked a lot like the fancy paddock boots Brooke had seen at the feed store.

Silly, Brooke told herself with a smile. *Mom's always saying how my horsey clothes are right in style. Kiersten probably got hers at the mall. She's probably never even seen a horse up close.*

Brooke's mind was drifting back to Foxy when Kiersten cleared her throat and started her report. Brooke blinked and sat up a little straighter when she heard the word "horse."

". . . the stable boy feeds the orphan foal with camel's milk," Kiersten was reading from the papers in her hand. "And thanks to his care, Sham grows big and strong and faster than any other horse in the sultan's stables. . . ."

That's more like it! Brooke thought.

She listened with interest as Kiersten continued her report. The new girl's voice was soft, but Brooke leaned forward so she could hear every word. The book she was talking about sounded interesting, and at the end Brooke was surprised to hear that it was by one of her favorite authors, Marguerite Henry.

When Kiersten sat down, Brooke watched her out of the corner of her eye, ignoring Hunter Webb's report on some dumb sports story. Had Kiersten chosen that book at random? Or because she was interested in history? Or could she be interested in horses just like Brooke?

Finally the bell rang to end class. Brooke gathered up her books and glanced back at Adam. He was horsing around with his friends again, so she decided to ask him about the jumps later.

Noticing Kiersten heading for the door, Brooke grabbed

the rest of her stuff and caught up with her. "Hey," she said, feeling a little shy. "I liked your book report. What was the name of the book again?"

Kiersten shot her a small smile in return. "Thanks. It's called *King of the Wind*."

Brooke nodded, making a mental note to look for it the next time she went to the library. "I've read a few other books by the same author, but not that one," she told Kiersten as the two of them stepped out into the crowded school hallway. "My favorite is *Misty of Chincoteague*."

Kiersten's smile was bigger this time. "Really? I love that one too!"

"So . . ." Brooke hugged her books to her chest, not sure how to ask the next question. "Um, do you just like horse books, or actual horses, too?"

Kiersten laughed. "Both," she said, her greenish-hazel eyes brightening. "I've been riding forever." Then her expression went sort of dim and distant again. "I mean, I used to ride—you know, up in Pennsylvania, before we moved here."

Something about the way Kiersten's mouth puckered

as she said the last part made Brooke feel awkward, as if Brooke had said something wrong without realizing it. "Pennsylvania?" Brooke blurted out, trying to cover her own discomfort. "My friend Nina has cousins who live there."

"Really?" Kiersten perked up again. "Where in Pennsylvania?"

"Um, I'm not sure." Brooke was already wishing she hadn't said anything. At least not about Nina. Adam was always telling her how weird it was that she considered the other Pony Post members close friends even though she'd never even met them in person. How was she supposed to explain something like that to someone she'd just met?

At that moment Adam burst out of the classroom and almost crashed into Brooke and Kiersten. He veered off just in time, tossing his hair off his forehead as his pale blue eyes barely grazed Brooke's face.

"Yo, B," he said, and then the twins caught up to him and the three of them ran off down the hall, pushing and shoving and laughing loudly.

What's happened to Adam lately, anyway? Brooke wondered uneasily, watching them go. *It's like he doesn't even remember we're friends anymore.*

It was a weird thought. Because she couldn't even remember a time when the two of them hadn't been friends—*best* friends. More like brother and sister, really. He was the only other kid near her age who lived within several miles of her house, which meant they'd only had each other to play with growing up. But that had been okay with both of them. They'd spent most of their time exploring every last corner of the woods, fields, and creeks near their homes, on foot or on their bikes. Then Foxy had come along, and they'd been able to explore even farther, with Brooke riding her pony and Adam on the fancy dirt bike he'd gotten for his tenth birthday.

Last spring all that had started to change, though. Brooke had noticed that Adam didn't always sit with her at lunch anymore, and he didn't come by after school as often either. That summer things had gotten even stranger. Instead of turning up at the screen door every morning, Adam had practically disappeared, spending most of his time with his swim team buddies or other boys Brooke barely knew. Sure, he still came to hang out sometimes. But not like before.

Brooke had discussed Adam's odd behavior with her Pony Post friends. Nina, who seemed to know the most about boys, had advised her to wait and see what happened. She said boys their age "went all weird sometimes" and that he'd probably go back to normal eventually. In the meantime it wouldn't do any good to worry about it. Maddie had agreed, pointing out that you couldn't really change other people—something Maddie's parents apparently liked to remind her of every time she complained about her prissy older sister or her rambunctious younger brothers.

Brooke was trying to follow her friends' advice. But it wasn't easy, and she sighed as she watched Adam disappear around the corner of the school hallway.

Oh well, she thought. *It's a good thing I have other friends.*

Suddenly remembering that Adam and his goony buddies had cut her and Kiersten off practically midsentence, she turned back to where the other girl had been standing. But Kiersten was gone.

Brooke bit her lip, feeling bad about spacing out on the new girl, and making a silent vow to try to talk to her again sometime. Brooke had discovered at camp that she wasn't very confident about making new friends—she'd never had to be, since most of the kids at her school had been going there since kindergarten, just like her and Adam. But maybe Kiersten would turn out to be worth a little extra effort. None of Brooke's other local friends had any interest in horses at all, aside from Adam, who sometimes helped her with Foxy's training or asked to hop on bareback for a quick ride.

Maybe I'll ask Maddie for tips on getting to know Kiersten better, Brooke thought. Maddie's mother was a sergeant in the US Air Force, which meant the family moved a lot. Brooke couldn't imagine having to get used to a new home and a new school every few years, though Maddie didn't seem to mind it too much.

Joining the stream of students pouring toward the exit, Brooke headed for her locker. After that she found herself swept out into a bitterly cold but sunny afternoon. The wind tickled her neck and she shivered. She hunched farther into the collar of her coat as she hurried toward the buses idling at the curb. As she climbed aboard hers she glanced around for Adam, but he was nowhere in sight.

That was no surprise. Ever since basketball tryouts had started a few days earlier, Adam had been staying after school almost every day.

Oh well, Brooke thought. *I'll have to call him later to talk about building some jumps.*

She found a seat near the front of the bus, already looking forward to spending the rest of the afternoon with Foxy.

◆ CHAPTER ◆

2

"BRR!" BROOKE EXCLAIMED AS SHE RUSHED
into her house, chased by a stray gust of wind. It was cold
out there—a lot colder than it had been that morning.

The house was quiet and dim. When she headed into
the kitchen, Brooke found a note from her mother on the
fridge saying she was at the grocery store.

*Good. That means she can't make me vacuum the liv-
ing room or something instead of going out to ride,* Brooke
thought, stepping to the back door and peering out. She
couldn't see Foxy from there, but she could see the wind
setting the trees dancing, and she shivered.

No need to rush right back outside, she figured. Her

mother probably had the twins with her, which meant she wasn't likely to be home for a while, since grocery shopping with two five-and-a-half-year-olds always seemed to take twice as long as it should. And if Brooke didn't let her fingers thaw before she headed out to the barn, she wouldn't even be able to groom her pony, let alone buckle the girth on her English saddle or hold the reins. . . .

She decided to have a snack while she was warming up. The twins had eaten all the cookies, and the peanut butter jar was empty, but Brooke found a slightly overripe banana in the bottom of the fruit basket. She wolfed it down, along with a glass of milk, then headed upstairs.

The door to her room was ajar, and there were a few pieces of Legos scattered just inside. Great. That meant Ethan and Emma had been there. Brooke tried to keep them out of her room, but her mom and stepdad refused to let her put a lock on her door, and the twins often "forgot" that they weren't supposed to go in there when they weren't invited.

Everything seemed to be where she'd left it, though, so she just kicked the Legos out into the hall and wandered over to the window. From there she could see Foxy standing near her water trough nibbling at the remnants of the hay pile Brooke had set out for her that morning before school. The pony had the three-acre pasture to herself, but just across the fence at the back of the property was the neighbors' much larger field, where several retired draft horses lived. Luckily the drafts' favorite spot to snooze was under the big oak tree along the fence line. Brooke was glad, since that meant Foxy usually had company while she grazed nearby.

Brooke smiled at the sight of her pony. She touched the window lightly with her fingertips, and then pulled them away quickly due to the chill on the glass. If she was going to ride today, she'd better put on a few more layers.

She headed over to her dresser and dug out an old wool hunting sweater of her stepfather's that had shrunk in the wash. The dark green color had faded, and it had a hole in one elbow, but it was the warmest item of clothing Brooke owned. She tossed the sweater onto her bed, along with a pair of thick socks and a fleece headband.

There. That should keep her warm enough to get a

good ride in despite the weather. She glanced at the window, still not quite ready to dive back out into the cold just yet.

Maybe the wind will die down if I give it a few more minutes, she thought. *Otherwise it might be too cold to ride today after all.*

She chewed her lower lip, wandering over to the window again to look out at Foxy. Her Pony Post friends wouldn't let a little cold weather stop them from their riding plans, would they? Especially Haley, who lived in Wisconsin and had already mentioned snow flurries in her latest posts.

Thinking about the other Pony Posters, Brooke grabbed her laptop. She might as well check the site while she was deciding what to do.

Soon she was cross-legged on her bed with her laptop open in front of her. She clicked the bookmark for the Pony Post, and within seconds the site's familiar logo popped up. It showed four Chincoteague ponies galloping through the surf. Nina had designed the image with help from her mother, who was an artist. But Brooke was the one who'd uploaded it onto the site, placed it, and resized it to fit perfectly at the top of the page. She had the most experience with computers out of the four of them, which was why they'd made her the webmaster of the Pony Post, even though the whole thing had been Maddie's idea in the first place.

Brooke scrolled down, but nobody had posted anything new since she'd checked in that morning. So she opened a new text box and started to type.

[BROOKE] Hi all! Happy Monday! Anyone here?

She sat back and waited, not really expecting a response. All four girls spent enough time on the site that it wasn't too unusual to log on and find one or more of the others there at the same time. On the other hand, they all had busy lives in different time zones. Brooke guessed that Maddie was definitely still at school, while the other two might still be on their way home—or on their way to see their own ponies.

But after just a few seconds, another post appeared:

[HALEY] I'm here! Hi, B. Did u ride today?

Brooke smiled, just the sight of her friend's name on the screen lifting her mood. She typed her response quickly.

[BROOKE] Not yet. I just got home from school a little while ago. I was thinking about skipping riding today b/c it's soooo cold out! But I think I'll have some hot cocoa and then at least hop on bareback for a few min. What about u?

[HALEY] Nope. Wings has the day off today. We don't usually ride on Mondays. But tomorrow if it doesn't snow too hard, we'll be back to work.

[BROOKE] Snow? Brr! And I thought it was cold here!!!

[HALEY] LOL, it'll prolly just be flurries. If it's not too windy I'll ride anyway. B/c guess what? I decided I want to be ready to enter

a real recognized event in the spring.

[BROOKE] Rly? Cool! I'm sure you'll be ready

by spring. U have been learning a lot lately,

right? Esp. in that clinic u did last month.

As she hit enter, Brooke heard high, chattering voices downstairs. Stepping over to the window, she saw her mother's SUV parked out front. The twins were chasing each other in and out of the house, while their mom was pulling a bag of groceries out of the back.

The computer pinged, and Brooke hurried back over to see what Haley had posted.

[HALEY] Def! That's what gave me the idea.

I've been thinking about it ever since then. But

after our great rides this weekend, I decided for

sure. I even know which event I want to enter.

It's the first one of the spring around here, and

it's at the same farm where I did the clinic.

Brooke glanced toward the door, feeling a little distracted. So much for getting her ride in before everyone got home. . . . Leaning over the keyboard, she typed quickly and posted.

> [BROOKE] That's good. U and Wings
>
> will already know yr way around. Oops!
>
> Mom just got home and has a car
>
> full of groceries to unload, so gtg—
>
> will check in later if I can. . . .

After closing the laptop, she hurried downstairs. Her mother was just coming in the front door with an overflowing grocery bag in each arm. The twins were in the entryway, yanking at their mittens and hats and boots, their cheeks pink from the cold.

"Oh, Brooke, good," Mrs. Rhodes said. "There's one more bag in the car. Can you grab it?" Without waiting for an answer, she hurried toward the kitchen, her heels click-clacking on the hardwood floor. She was a real estate agent and wore heels, makeup, and nice clothes everywhere she went, in case she ran into a client or got called in for an important showing.

"Brooke, Brooke!" Ethan was half in and half out of his puffy down jacket, and he almost tripped over his loose sleeve as he jumped up and down and smacked Brooke on the arm. "Guess what?"

"What?" Brooke dodged his hand and headed for the door.

"I'll tell her!" Emma yelled.

"No, me! It was my idea!" Ethan argued back.

Brooke ignored them, darting outside and pushing the door shut behind her. She hadn't bothered to put her coat on, and the cold wrapped itself around her immediately as she rushed over and grabbed a heavy bag of groceries out of the SUV.

When she got back inside, the twins were waiting. "I rode a horse!" Ethan announced loudly.

"He-e-e-ey!" Emma wailed, clenching her fists. "I was gonna tell her!"

"Too bad, so sad," Ethan sing-songed.

Brooke rolled her eyes. "Too bad, so sad" was one of

her stepfather's favorite phrases, though she suspected her mother wouldn't be thrilled to discover that the twins had picked up on it.

Then she realized what her little brother had said. "Wait, what do you mean?" she asked. "What horse?"

"The one at the grocery store," Ethan told her proudly. "I rode it twice!"

Now Brooke realized what they were talking about. There was a mechanical pony in front of the grocery store that rocked back and forth when you put a quarter into the slot. It had been there forever, and Brooke had loved riding it when she was the twins' age.

"Me too," Emma shouted. "I rode too."

"Yeah, but I rode like a real cowboy." Ethan puffed out his chest.

Their mother bustled back into the entryway. "Brooke, the groceries?"

"Coming." Brooke dodged around the twins and followed her mother into the kitchen.

She was putting away some crackers when Ethan and Emma came rushing in, sliding on the tile floor in their stocking feet. They'd left their boots and most of their other outdoor clothes in the entryway, though Emma was still wearing her favorite pink knit hat with the mouse ears on it.

Ethan slid right into Brooke, catching his balance by grabbing her elbow. "I told you I'm a cowboy," he said, grinning up at her. "I proved it! So now you have to let me ride Foxy."

"Me too!" Emma put in. "I want to ride Foxy too!"

Brooke sighed. The twins had watched some old Western on TV the week before, and Ethan had thought he was a cowboy ever since. He'd been bugging her off and on about riding Foxy, though she'd pretty much ignored the requests.

"Let's go ride now!" Ethan started galloping around the kitchen, pretending to whip his imaginary horse. "Come on, come on! I'm a cowboy!"

"Me too, me too!" Emma followed her brother, giggling wildly.

"Forget it." Brooke had to raise her voice to be heard over the din. "It's too cold. Besides, Foxy isn't a cow pony; she's a Chincoteague pony."

Ethan stopped short, looking wounded. "She is so! She's a cow pony. And I want to ride 'em cowboy!"

"Ride 'em cowgirl!" Emma yelled, waving her arms and sending a package of pasta crashing off the counter onto the floor.

Brooke's mother had been busy unpacking produce and putting it into the crisper, but now she turned and glanced at the twins with a sigh. "Brooke," she said. "Why don't you take them out and give them a quick pony ride, hmm?"

"What?" Brooke stared at her.

"Just this once." Her mother sounded a little impatient as she click-clacked over to grab the fallen box of pasta. "I'm sure a quick ride will get it out of their systems."

"But I was just about to ride Foxy myself," Brooke protested.

"Perfect." Her mother smiled. "We'll just pop the twins on first, and then Foxy will be all ready for you to have your ride afterward."

"But—" Brooke began, but she was quickly drowned out by Ethan's and Emma's shrieks and shouts of glee.

They stamped for the back door, already arguing about who got to ride first.

"Hold it right there," their mother called out. "Coats and boots back on first." She shot Brooke a distracted smile. "Thanks for doing this, sweetie. Better bundle up yourself, hmm?"

"Stop!" Brooke grabbed Ethan by the arm as he started to dart around Foxy's rump. "Don't walk behind the pony, remember?"

"Yeah, dummy." Emma stuck her tongue out at her brother. "Foxy'll kick your head off!"

"No she won't." Ethan gave Foxy a hearty pat on the stomach, making the pony flinch and flick an ear back toward him. "Foxy loves me, 'cause I'm a real cowboy. And a cowboy's best friend is his trusty horse."

Brooke sighed. Foxy was tied to the fence near her water trough, and Brooke was doing her best to groom and tack her up quickly—the sooner the pony was ready, the sooner this would be over with.

But the twins weren't making it easy to get anything

done. First Emma had insisted on spending a good ten minutes brushing the pony's long, thick tail, even though it hadn't been tangled. Meanwhile Ethan had run off with Brooke's hoofpick to scratch in the mud under the trough. By the time Brooke had gotten it back, wiped it off, and cleaned out the pony's feet, Ethan had managed to knock over the grooming bucket, spilling brushes, cloths, and curries everywhere.

Brooke had gritted her teeth as she'd gathered everything back up. Normally she loved grooming her pony, but today she figured Foxy wouldn't mind if she just knocked off the worst of the dirt to speed things along.

"Okay, she's clean enough." Brooke tossed her brush into the grooming bucket, then glanced at her mother, who was leaning against the fence nearby checking her cell phone. "Can you try to keep them from harassing Foxy too much while I grab my Western saddle?"

"Of course." Her mother sounded unconcerned, watching as Ethan and Emma started climbing around on the wooden fence.

Brooke shot the twins a slightly anxious glance, thanking her lucky stars that Foxy was so good-tempered. Then

Brooke darted into the glorified shed she called her barn. It was divided into what Brooke had dubbed the pony part and the people part. The pony part was just a three-sided area where Foxy could come in out of the weather, and where her feed and water buckets hung. Normally Brooke groomed and tacked in there too, but she'd decided that such close quarters might not be a good idea with her little siblings involved.

The people part of the barn was where Brooke kept Foxy's feed, tack, and other equipment. Her two saddles sat on a rack her stepfather had built, with her bridle hanging off the horn of the Western saddle.

Slinging the bridle over her shoulder, she grabbed the Western saddle and a pad. When she emerged back outside, she was surprised to find that the twins were nowhere in sight. For a second her heart lifted. The two of them had short attention spans. Could they have lost interest and decided they didn't want to ride after all?

Then she heard excited voices and looked over to see Ethan and Emma mobbing Adam, who had just pulled into the backyard on his dirt bike.

"Yo, twinsies," he greeted them with a laugh, lifting one arm so that Ethan's feet dangled several inches off the ground. "What's up?"

Now Brooke was even more surprised. What was Adam doing here? She was pretty sure he was supposed to have basketball tryouts all afternoon. A year ago she wouldn't have hesitated to ask what was going on, but given the way things had been between them lately, she felt a little shy.

Her mother, however, wasn't shy at all. "Hello, Adam," she said. "How are basketball tryouts going?"

"Oh. Uh, not so hot, actually." Adam turned away, fiddling with the kickstand on his bike. "I got cut today," he mumbled over his shoulder.

"Oh dear." Brooke's mother clucked sympathetically. "But you've always been so athletic!"

"Yeah, well . . ." Adam shrugged, then grabbed Emma and spun her around, making her shriek and giggle.

Brooke could tell he didn't want to talk about it, and no wonder. He'd been really excited about making the team. She decided she'd better change the subject before her mother started grilling him.

"Hey, want to help with Foxy?" Brooke asked him. "The twins want to go for a pony ride."

"Not a pony ride, a cowboy ride!" Ethan corrected. He immediately started telling Adam all about the movie he'd seen and the mechanical horse at the store.

Adam wandered over to Foxy as he listened. He gave the pony a pat on the neck, and she nuzzled him, clearly looking for one of the peppermints he sometimes brought her from his dad's restaurant.

"Okay, pardner," Adam said at last in a mock Western drawl, interrupting Ethan's excited description of how hard the mechanical horse had bucked. "Cowboys are all about ridin', not talkin'. So let's get this here cow pony saddled up, okay?"

He reached for the Western saddle, which Brooke had set on the fence. "Do you remember how to do the cinch?" she asked as he swung it onto Foxy's back.

"Course I do." He grinned at her. "I was the one who helped you figure it out, remember?"

She did remember. She'd found the Western saddle at a garage sale before Foxy had even been old enough for

Brooke to ride her. The first time Brooke had tried to put it on the pony, Brooke hadn't been able to work out how to tie the Western cinch, which was much different from the English girths she'd used up until then. Adam had done a little research on the Internet and had almost immediately been able to catch on to how the cinch knot worked, thanks mostly to learning all kinds of different knots from his grandpa when they took his fishing boat out in the Chesapeake Bay. Brooke had had a little more trouble getting the hang of it, but Adam had demonstrated over and over again until she'd finally mastered it, not even teasing her—much—about her fumble fingers.

Brooke didn't ride Western much anymore, preferring either her English saddle or bareback, so she stood back and let him tie the cinch, figuring he'd get it done faster.

"Ready," he said, snugging it up tight. "Who's first?"

"Me! Me! Me!" the twins cried in unison, jumping up and down and waving their hands.

Adam bent and picked up a stone off the ground. "Okay, here's how we'll decide," he said, putting both hands behind his back. Then he held them out, both hands closed into fists. "Whoever picks the hand with the stone in it goes first. That's the cowboy way, right? So no arguing, pardners."

Luckily, the twins each chose a different hand, and when Adam opened his fists, the stone was in the one Ethan had picked.

"Hooray!" Ethan yelled, making Foxy snort and turn her head to eye him warily.

"No yelling," Brooke told her little brother. "Come on, let's get you up."

"I've got him." Adam grabbed Ethan under the arms and swung him into the saddle in one motion. Brooke was a little surprised that he could do that. When had he gotten so tall?

Just then Brooke's mother looked up from her phone. "Be careful, honey," she called to Ethan. "Do what Brooke and Adam say, all right?"

Ethan ignored her, grabbing the horn and leaning forward. "Where's the reins?" he demanded.

"No reins." Brooke untied Foxy's lead rope from the fence, leaving the bridle hanging on the gate. "I'm going to lead her while Adam walks next to you. Okay?" She glanced at Adam.

"Sure." Adam patted Ethan on the leg. "Come on, pardner. Let's go ride the range."

Ethan giggled, seeming to forget about not having reins, and Brooke breathed out a sigh of relief. "Come on, Foxy," she whispered, clucking to the mare. "This won't take long. . . ."

"Again! Again!" Ethan cried as Brooke led Foxy back to the fence after leading Emma around the field.

Brooke sighed and sneaked a peek at her watch. The twins' pony rides had been going on for almost an hour. After Ethan had gotten off, Emma had taken her turn. Then Ethan had decided he wanted Adam to take pictures of him riding, so he'd climbed on again, and Adam had snapped a few shots with his smartphone.

Naturally, Emma had wanted pictures too. She'd posed enthusiastically, even trying to stand up in the saddle before Brooke had stopped her.

And now Ethan wanted another turn and wasn't being

shy about letting them know. Brooke's mother had wandered into the house for a cup of coffee a few minutes earlier, but now she returned.

"Oh, let them each have one more turn," she told Brooke, sipping at her steaming mug. "They're having so much fun."

Brooke sighed. "Sure, why not." Actually, she had to admit it was fun to see her little sister and brother enjoying Foxy so much. So what if they were rapidly running out of daylight for her own ride? It was probably too cold to do much real work anyway, since afterward she'd have to walk Foxy until she was fully cooled out, and that would mean even more time out in the cold.

Soon Ethan was back on board. This time he started kicking as soon as Brooke set off on her circuit around the pasture.

"Hey, when do I get to gallop?" he said. "I want to gallop!"

"No galloping. Sorry," Brooke said.

Ethan pouted. "But all cowboys gallop! I can do it."

"Well, Foxy can't," Brooke told him. "For one thing, the ground's too hard this time of year."

Adam was still walking alongside the pony, his glove-less hands shoved into the pockets of his jeans. "We could let him try a little trot, though," he suggested. "How's that sound, buddy?"

"Yeah! Trot, trot!" Ethan exclaimed, instantly excited again.

Brooke frowned. She wasn't sure trotting was a good idea. The twins were pretty wobbly up there, and they weren't even wearing helmets. Still, she didn't want to argue with Adam when he was being so nice.

"Okay, I guess," she said. "But you lead and I'll jog beside him, okay?"

"Sure." They traded places, and Adam clucked to Foxy. "Come on, girl—let's go!"

The mare took a few quick walk steps, then surged into a trot. "Easy," Brooke called, grabbing her little brother's knee to stop him from toppling off the far side of the saddle.

Ethan giggled, thumping both legs on the mare's sides again and almost kicking Brooke in the face in the process. "Faster, faster!" he yelled.

"Stop kicking," Brooke ordered. "She's going fast enough."

They trotted halfway to the opposite fence line and back. After that, Emma wanted a turn at the faster gait. She was a little more nervous than her brother, clutching the horn tightly as the pony started trotting. But after a few seconds she was giggling.

"I'm galloping!" she squealed, letting go of the horn and waving her hands over her head like someone on a roller coaster. "We're running like the wind!"

Brooke smiled distractedly, her mind flashing to Kiersten's book report on *King of the Wind*. Then she tuned back in as she saw Emma tipping backward.

"Sit up," she said, reaching up to steady her sister as Adam glanced back and brought Foxy to a walk again.

"Everything okay back there?" he asked.

"Go again!" Emma insisted. "I want to do it again."

Brooke wanted to tell Adam to ignore her, that it was time for the pony rides to be over. But once again she held her tongue. As long as Brooke stayed right beside her, Emma would be fine, and another brief trot certainly wouldn't hurt Foxy any. Besides, this was the most time she and Adam had spent together in ages—and if the pony rides ended, he might decide to go home.

"Okay," Brooke said, taking a tighter grip on her sister's leg. "One more time . . ."

The pony rides continued until Brooke's stepfather arrived home twenty minutes later. As soon as they saw him, the twins ran over, shouting over each other in their eagerness to tell him all about their adventures. The three of them headed inside, along with Brooke's mother, leaving Brooke and Adam with Foxy.

"That was fun," Adam said with a smile. "I forgot what a riot the twins can be."

"Yeah, well, you don't have to live with them," Brooke muttered, stepping over to loosen Foxy's cinch.

Adam chuckled. "You going to ride now?"

"Nah, it's getting dark." Brooke had warmed up a little while jogging alongside the pony, but now her teeth were starting to chatter again.

Adam squinted up at the sky, which was going shades

of purple and orange as the sun set. "Yeah, guess so. Here, I'll get the saddle."

With his help Brooke got Foxy untacked and settled into the pony part of the barn with her dinner. By the time they'd finished, it was almost fully dark. Leaving the pony with her face buried in her feed bucket, the two of them wandered outside and leaned on the gate, watching the shadowy shapes of the draft horses on the far side of the field.

"Thanks for helping out today." Brooke shot him a look. She wanted to say something about the basketball team but didn't quite dare; Adam could be funny about stuff like that sometimes. "Actually, I'm glad you came by," she said instead. "I wanted to talk to you about something. . . ."

She quickly explained about her plans to start jumping more, and asked if he'd help her build some jumps. He nodded immediately.

"Sounds good," he said. "I went mountain biking at this place where they also do horse stuff, and I saw a bunch of really interesting jumps. There was one shaped like a triangle, and a boxy one with sticks glued to it. Maybe we could make some cool stuff like that."

"Those might have been cross-country jumps," Brooke guessed. "That's what Haley does."

"Who?" Then he grinned. "Wait, that's one of your imaginary friends, right?"

Brooke stuck out her tongue at him, and just like that, things were back to normal between them. They chatted about their jump-building plans until it got too cold to stay out there anymore. Brooke waved good-bye as he pedaled off on his bike, and then she hurried inside, hoping her fingers weren't too frozen to type, since she couldn't wait to tell her Pony Post friends all about her day.

◆ CHAPTER ◆
3

AFTER LUNCH THE NEXT DAY BROOKE STOPPED by her locker to pick up her books for her afternoon classes. She'd just swung open the metal locker door when she saw Kiersten coming down the crowded hallway.

The new girl saw her, too, and walked over. "Hi," she said, glancing toward Brooke's locker. "Cute pony. Is it yours?"

"Yeah, that's Foxy." Brooke followed her gaze to the photo taped up inside the locker door. Adam had taken it last winter—it showed Brooke sitting on Foxy bareback, leaning down to hug the mare's fuzzy neck. "It's kind of a silly picture, but I like it."

Kiersten leaned closer. "No, it's adorable. What kind of pony is Foxy?"

"She's a Chincoteague."

"Really? Cool!" Kiersten smiled. "Just like Misty of Chincoteague, right? You know, like we were talking about yesterday?"

"Yeah. Reading that book over and over was what made me want to get a Chincoteague pony of my own," Brooke admitted.

Kiersten smiled. "Awesome. Did you get her at the pony auction? It takes place pretty close to here, right?"

Brooke nodded. "Chincoteague's about an hour away. And yes, that's where I got her."

"That's amazing." Kiersten leaned against the lockers, clutching her books to her chest. "What was it like?"

Brooke smiled and closed her eyes for a second, drifting back to that day. "It was the best day of my life." She opened her eyes and glanced at Kiersten. "I'd been bugging my parents for ages to let me go down there and buy a pony. I couldn't believe it when they finally said yes!"

She went on to tell the other girl all about it—how

they'd arrived early to watch the ponies swim across the channel between Assateague and Chincoteague Islands, and how once the herd was in the corrals on the Chincoteague side, Brooke had spent the rest of the afternoon wandering around picking out which young ponies she wanted to bid on at the auction the next day. She'd spent the night in the B and B dreaming of training and riding and taking care of a sweet spotted pony of her very own—one that looked just like the famous Misty of Chincoteague.

The trouble was, all the young ponies that looked like Misty had sold for much more than Brooke could afford. Toward the end of the auction, it had been Foxy's turn on the auction block. Brooke had noticed the cute flaxen chestnut filly's quiet temperament in the pens, though Brooke hadn't put Foxy on her list, since she wasn't a pinto like Misty. Still, Brooke had liked the way the gangly little yearling had stood calmly watching the crowd, and so Brooke had raised her hand as the auctioneer had called for bids. But even after she'd bid all she could, others had still seemed interested, and Brooke had been afraid she'd end up going home with no pony at all—until her stepfather had raised his hand, adding a hundred dollars of his money to Brooke's so she could win Foxy.

"Wow," Kiersten said when Brooke had finished the story. "That's so cool."

Brooke nodded, opening her mouth to tell Kiersten about the Pony Post. But just then the bell rang, signaling that classes were starting again.

"Oops," Brooke said, quickly rummaging around for her books. "I don't want to be late."

"Me neither." Kiersten grinned. "The teachers are still cutting me some slack since I'm the new girl, but I don't want to push it."

Brooke laughed and waved as the two of them hurried off in opposite directions. Only when she was at her desk in her science classroom did Brooke realize that she still hadn't found out anything about Kiersten's horse experience.

Oh well, she thought. *I'll have to ask her about that next time.*

When Brooke walked into the kitchen that afternoon, her mother was sitting at the table sipping coffee and typing on her laptop. The rest of the house was quiet.

"Hi," Brooke said, stepping over to the refrigerator to grab a snack. "Where is everybody?"

Her mother glanced up. "The twins are at a playdate, and your father's at the lot. I'll be off in a sec myself—I have a showing."

"Okay." Brooke was relieved to hear that the twins weren't home. They'd had so much fun riding Foxy yesterday that she'd been afraid they might want to do it again.

She glanced at her mother, wondering if she should say something about that. Foxy was her pony, and the mare was still young and a little green. One of Brooke's old riding instructors had once told her that every time you rode a horse, you were either training it or untraining it. She didn't like the idea of the twins deciding they could hop on and ride any old time, since she doubted what they did up there could be considered training.

Just then her mother checked her watch, took one last sip of coffee, and jumped to her feet. "I'm out of here," she said briskly, straightening the lapels of her navy-blue blazer. "Wish me luck. Business has been slow lately, with all the cold weather, and I could really use this commission."

"Good luck." Brooke decided not to bother talking to her mother about the twins, at least right now. For one thing, it was obvious her mother was already focused on her showing. Besides, what were the odds that the short-attention-span twins would actually want to ride again?

Once her mother had gone, Brooke headed for the stairs, planning to check in with the Pony Post before going out to the barn to wait for Adam. Halfway up the stairs, she heard the doorbell chime.

It was Adam. "Hey," Brooke greeted him in surprise. "Since when do you come to the front door?"

Adam grinned and shrugged. "Just come on. I looked up some pictures of jump plans during study hall today, and I have some ideas. . . ."

A few minutes later they were dragging tools and two-by-fours out of the shed behind the garage. After hearing about the jump-building project, Brooke's stepfather had told her she could use anything she wanted from in there. It was where he stuck all the stuff he didn't have any particular use for but didn't want to throw away, and it was a treasure trove of scrap lumber, stray hardware, loose screws and nails, half-empty cans of paint, and random semi-broken tools. The weather was a little warmer than it had been for the past couple of days, so instead of working in the garage as they'd planned, they decided to set up their tools and materials on the frostbitten grass right outside Foxy's pasture.

"That way we won't have to carry the stuff as far once it's done," Adam said, dropping a stack of boards onto the ground next to the tool bag he'd brought.

"Sounds good." Brooke was glad that he seemed to be in a cheerful mood. She'd been afraid he might be mopey after getting cut from the basketball team. She was sure she would have been feeling pretty blue if something like that had happened to her.

But she wasn't going to complain, that was for sure. It was almost feeling like old times, the two of them together and getting started on a fun project. Like all his weird behavior over the past six months had never happened at all. Brooke liked the feeling.

Once they were set up, it didn't take long to build two sets of jump standards and a small coop. That was one of the jumps Adam had researched online. It was a triangular jump, sort of like an A-frame shelter for chickens. As she held a piece of wood steady so Adam could screw it into place, Brooke made a mental note to take a picture of her new jumps to show the Pony Post. She was sure they'd be interested—especially Haley, who had built all the jumps in her cross-country schooling field, with some help from her uncle and cousins.

Adam kept up a steady chatter as they worked, talking about school, their families, and various other topics, though he didn't mention basketball at all. After a while Foxy noticed the two of them working and wandered over to watch them over the fence, between nibbles of dry grass.

Finally Adam hammered one last nail into the coop, stepped back, and brushed off his hands. "Okay, that should be enough to get you started," he said, sounding pleased with their work. "We can paint them another time if you want. For now let's bring them in, and then how about you and Foxy give it a try?"

"What—you mean jump right now?" Brooke couldn't help feeling startled. Somehow she hadn't thought much past this building project. Now her heart thumped as she stared at the coop, which suddenly looked much bigger than it had a second ago. Were she and Foxy really ready to get back to serious jumping?

"Go on and throw on that English saddle of yours," Adam urged. "I can't wait to see Foxy go. I'm sure she's going to be a jumping superstar!"

"Yeah, she is." Brooke flashed back to summer camp, where Foxy had done really well over fences, especially considering her lack of experience. She'd even won some ribbons at the little end-of-camp show, and the camp's owner, a very experienced show jumper, had mentioned more than once that she thought the pony had natural talent. Remembering that made Brooke feel a little more excited about seeing what Foxy could do over their new jumps.

By the time she'd caught Foxy and had done a quick grooming and saddling, Adam had dragged all the new stuff into the corner of the pasture that served as Brooke's main riding area. He was settling one of the wooden poles that had already been in there into the notches they'd made in the standards, when Brooke led the pony toward him.

"Put that a little lower, okay?" she said. "We should start with— Hey, Foxy, what's wrong? Easy, girl!"

The mare was backing up to the end of the reins, head high and eyes rolling as she stared toward the riding area. Brooke realized that Foxy had just noticed the new jumps, and like most horses, she could be a little nervous about anything new. That was another memory from camp, actually. When they'd first arrived, Foxy had acted more like a wild mustang fresh off the range than the calm, steady pony she normally was.

"What's with her?" Adam glanced over his shoulder at Foxy. "She's totally spazzing out."

"She'll be okay." Brooke talked soothingly to Foxy. She waited until Foxy had settled a bit, and then gave a gentle tug on the reins to lead her forward again. "She'll probably calm down once I get on."

Brooke pulled down her stirrups and quickly swung aboard. But as she settled into the saddle, she could feel that Foxy was still tense. When Brooke stuck her foot into the off-side stirrup, the mare jumped and spun around, almost causing Brooke to lose her balance.

"Whoa, Foxy—settle down!" Brooke quickly gathered up the reins, trying to get Foxy's attention back on her. She glanced at Adam. "I'm not sure we're going to be able to actually jump anything today. Maybe I should just let her walk around and get used to the new stuff."

"Oh, I'm sure she'll be fine in a minute," Adam said. "You're brave, right, Foxy?"

Brooke smiled tightly, steering the mare a little closer to one of the new jumps. Foxy kept a wary eye on it, side-stepping when they passed it.

After a few circles around the jumps, Foxy seemed calmer. But Brooke could tell she was still nervous.

"Go ahead. Try a jump now," Adam called from where he was perched on the pasture fence watching them.

Brooke hesitated, knowing that he was eager to see the results of all their hard work. She wasn't quite comfortable with how Foxy was feeling. "I have an idea," she said. "Can you take one of the rails down and put it on the ground between the standards? Then I'll try to get her to step over it—you know, to get her used to the idea."

Adam looked dubious, but he shrugged and went over to one of the fences. Foxy startled in place when he dropped one of the wooden rails to the ground, letting out a snort in reaction to the loud *thunking* sound the rail made.

"It's okay, girl." Brooke reached forward and stroked the pony's neck. "You can do this."

She urged Foxy forward. A few steps out, the mare tried to stop, and for a second Brooke was tempted to let her. But she channeled her Pony Post friends, trying to be brave like they were.

"Walk on, Foxy!" she said sternly, closing both legs on the mare's sides.

The pony let out another snort but finally skittered forward, half-stepping and half-hopping over the rail and then trotting away with her head held high.

"I think that's enough for today," Brooke called to Adam, feeling a little breathless as she wrestled Foxy to a walk and then turned her around.

"Are you kidding? She hasn't even jumped anything yet!" Adam stepped toward them. "Want me to get on?"

"You want to ride her?" Brooke was surprised. It had been a long time since Adam had expressed any interest in riding. "Um . . ."

"Come on. What's the worst that could happen?" He grinned and grabbed Foxy by the bridle. "Hop off and let me take her for a spin."

Still feeling a little uncertain, Brooke dismounted and helped Adam lengthen the stirrups on her English saddle. Then she watched as he swung aboard and clucked to Foxy, sending her trotting off before he'd even bothered to gather up the reins.

She held her breath as he turned her toward the second set of jump standards, which he'd set up as a crossrail. Would Foxy freak out, refuse the jump, maybe even spook so hard that Adam fell off? If she did, would he stop coming around again?

To Brooke's surprise, however, her pony's ears were pricked and her trot was mostly steady as she neared the crossrail. Two or three strides out she hesitated, trying to veer off to the left. But Adam growled at her and gave her a kick, and just like that—Foxy surged forward and leaped over the jump!

"Wow!" Brooke exclaimed as Foxy landed and cantered off nicely. "That looked great!"

Adam grinned at her over his shoulder. "Told you she's a superstar. Let's try the coop next, Foxy."

Brooke watched with amazement as they hopped over several more jumps. Adam didn't exactly have the finesse of the girls Brooke had ridden with at camp. But he was athletic enough to manage the basics, and more important, he was confident, which seemed to make Foxy feel confident too.

Finally he brought the pony to a halt in front of Brooke, still grinning. "Okay, your turn again," he said. "Ready to give it another try?"

"Sure, I guess." Brooke felt a shiver of nerves up and down her spine. But she tamped them down as she remounted. She'd just seen how important it was to give her pony a confident ride. She had to do that too.

Foxy didn't feel tense anymore, which helped Brooke

relax. She aimed the pony at the crossrail, holding her breath as they trotted toward it.

"Kick her if you have to," Adam called. "Don't let her slow down!"

Nodding, Brooke released her breath and gave the pony a nudge with both heels. "Go on, girl," she whispered.

Foxy flicked an ear back, then pricked it forward again—and jumped the crossrail as if she'd been doing it forever. Brooke smiled, then turned the pony toward the coop.

When Brooke entered the house half an hour later, she was still smiling. Who knew all it took was a little confidence to get Foxy to jump like that? She couldn't wait to tell the Pony Post all about it.

Unfortunately, she soon discovered that she had no way to do that, at least not at the moment. "Sorry, Brooke," her stepfather said when she asked if he'd seen her laptop. He was sitting at the kitchen table poring over some paperwork from the used car lot while Brooke's mother bustled around making dinner. "The twins are obsessed with some new online game and wouldn't stop fighting, so I told Emma she could play on your laptop while the E-man hogs the desktop."

Brooke's mother glanced at her. "You don't mind, do you, sweetie? It's so peaceful and quiet with them both busy."

"Sure, no problem." Brooke decided she'd rather take a shower before dinner anyway. Filling her friends in could wait.

✦ CHAPTER ✦
4

ON WEDNESDAY MORNING BROOKE WOKE
up a few minutes before the alarm was set to go off. When
she left her bedroom to go to the bathroom, she noticed
that someone had left her laptop on the floor outside her
door. She grabbed it and ducked back into her room, glad
to have a few extra minutes to update the Pony Post at last.

After logging on to the Internet, she saw her e-mail
icon blinking, so she clicked on that first. There was a new
message from Adam:

I'll come after school again today to
help u with the jumps. O and here

are some of the pix I took of the

twins riding the other day—lol!

Brooke clicked on the attachments, bringing up the photos. She couldn't help smiling at the sweet, patient look on Foxy's face in all of them, no matter what the twins were doing up on her back.

Remembering that she'd promised her Pony Post friends some pictures of the pony rides, she uploaded Adam's photos to the site as soon as she logged on. Then she settled down to see what her friends had posted since she'd checked in last.

The first post was from Nina, just telling them all about a movie she'd seen last night that had a horse in it.

The second post was from Maddie. And when Brooke scanned it, she gasped out loud.

"Oh no!" she murmured, wondering if she was reading it wrong. But when she read it again more slowly, it said the same thing.

[MADDIE] You guys aren't going to believe

this—I was snooping in my parents' office on

Mon. and I saw something I wasn't supposed to. It was 6 plane tix to London. As in England. I think the air force is transferring Mom again—all the way overseas this time! She hasn't breathed a word yet, but what else could those tix mean?!?!?!? Am I going to have to leave Cloudy behind in just a couple of months?!?!?!?!?!?!!? ☹☹☹☹☹☹

There was more, but Brooke could hardly take in the details. Maddie was moving to London? A whole ocean away from her favorite pony? Brooke opened a new text box and typed quickly.

[BROOKE] O wow, M, I'm so sorry! I can't believe this! Are you sure about what u saw? What did your parents say when u asked them about it? Is the move definite, or is there any possibility it might not happen?

She pressed enter, and her post appeared on the screen. Brooke just sat there staring at it for a moment, wishing she could talk to Maddie right now. But it was early, which meant the other Pony Posters were all probably still sound asleep—especially Maddie, who was three whole hours behind East Coast time.

Then again, I'd probably never be able to sleep again if I found out I had to move and leave Foxy behind, Brooke thought.

The very idea made her shudder—and not only because of Foxy. Brooke had lived in the same house since she was five, and the same county even before that. She couldn't imagine moving far away—especially to a whole other country!

Maybe having to deal with the twins riding Foxy isn't the worst thing in the world after all, she thought.

Just then the alarm started beeping loudly, making her jump. Time to get ready for school. She'd have to check in on Maddie later.

◆ ◆ ◆

Later that day Brooke was walking to the cafeteria with a couple of friends when she noticed Kiersten getting a drink at the water fountain nearby. Brooke paused, wondering if she should invite the new girl to sit with them at lunch. Maybe that would give Brooke a chance to ask about Kiersten's experience with horses, since she'd been too busy talking about Foxy to ask her anything yesterday.

"Brooke!" Adam's excited voice interrupted her thoughts. He was racing down the hall toward her, dodging clumps of wandering students. "Hold up!"

"Go on. I'll catch up in a sec," Brooke told the other girls, who nodded and continued toward the cafeteria.

When Adam reached her, he was grinning. "Listen, I have a great idea."

"What?" Brooke was more focused on the fact that he was actually talking to her at school than on whatever he wanted to tell her.

He rubbed his hands together. "I heard about this horse show," he began.

"Horse show?" That got Brooke's attention.

"Yeah. It's a week from Saturday. I guess it's, like, the

final local show of the season or something. You know, because it's almost winter? But it'll have tons of classes for beginning horses and ponies and riders and stuff. Plus it's at that farm over on Creek Road. Really close, right?"

"Oh." Brooke was vaguely aware of the place he was talking about. It was a small boarding barn a couple of miles from her house that sometimes hosted little shows and playdays. Brooke had gone to watch a few shows with her parents when she was little. "So do you want to go watch the show?" she asked Adam.

"Watch?" His grin widened. "I want you and Foxy to *enter*!"

"Enter?" Brooke blinked at him.

"Yeah. It's open to whoever wants to do it. I figured you could sign up for some of the beginner horse classes, since Foxy's still young and all. There's also something called equitation, which I think is, like, a contest for who rides the best or something?"

"Yeah, equitation is judged on the rider only, not the horse." Brooke gulped. "But listen, Foxy and I aren't really ready to show right now. I mean, we just started jumping again—you know, yesterday. And besides that, we've only ever done one show together."

"The one at camp, right?" Adam nodded. "And you told me you guys totally rocked that one!"

"We did." Brooke shrugged. "But that was different. I'm just not sure—"

Adam glanced down the hall, where several of his basketball buddies had just appeared. "Look, just think about it, okay?" he interrupted. "But you have to decide soon. Like I said, it's Saturday after next."

He started to hurry away. "Okay. I'll let you know after school," Brooke called after him.

When she got home, Brooke headed straight upstairs to check the Pony Post. Haley and Nina had added worried comments about Maddie's big news, but there were no updates yet from Maddie herself.

"She's probably still at school," Brooke murmured, remembering the time difference.

Her hands hovered over the keyboard as she wondered whether to tell her friends about the show Adam wanted her to enter. But she ended up logging off without posting anything at all, deciding that news could wait. For one thing, she didn't want to take away from Maddie's big problem. Besides that, she still hadn't decided whether to do the show or not. If she didn't, why even mention it at all?

Feeling oddly guilty, she hurried out to the barn. Foxy was nibbling at some leftover hay right outside her shed, so Brooke just let her stand there loose as she groomed her, knocking some dried mud off her fuzzy coat and picking out her hooves.

By the time she had the pony saddled, Adam had showed up. "Well?" he said expectantly.

Brooke turned away to slip the bridle over Foxy's head, still not sure what to say. A show could be fun, and this one was close enough to ride to without even needing to ask her stepfather to hook up the trailer. How often did a chance like that come along? And Adam was so excited about it. It could be a fun way to spend more time together.

Then again, she and Foxy didn't have much experience with showing. Hardly any, really. Even the thought of it made butterflies dance in Brooke's stomach.

"I'm not sure yet," she told him at last. "Ask me again after we ride, okay?"

"Sure." He looked slightly impatient but didn't argue. "I'll go set up the jumps while you get on."

Brooke mounted and rode out toward her makeshift arena. This time Foxy barely glanced at the jumps as Brooke walked and trotted her around to warm up.

"Looking good!" Adam called as she passed at a brisk trot. "When are you going to jump?"

"I guess we're ready now." Brooke brought the pony to a halt. "Can you put that second one a little lower?"

Adam obeyed, and when the jump was ready, Brooke trotted Foxy toward it. The pony hesitated slightly when she got close, but Brooke thought back to the day before and urged her forward. The hesitation made the pony's jump a little awkward, and her hind hoof clunked on the rail, sending it clattering to the ground. But when Brooke aimed her at the other crossrail, the pony jumped much better, clearing it with room to spare.

"Great!" Adam said. "You know, my buddy said he's watched his sister at a couple of these shows, and most of the people there look like they can hardly ride." He grinned. "You and Foxy will probably clean up. You know—if you do it."

"Yeah, okay." Brooke urged her pony forward again. "I should probably canter her before we try the coop. . . ."

The ride went well after that. Foxy spurted forward at the canter, tossing her head a little, but then she settled down and loped in a big circle around the jumps. It felt natural to turn her toward the coop when they passed it—and for Foxy to clear it with at least half a foot to spare.

"Whee!" Brooke exclaimed, laughing as they landed and cantered away. "Okay, that felt more like some of the jumps we did at camp." She brought the pony back to a walk and patted her. "I guess it's all coming back to you now, huh, Foxy?"

"That looked awesome!" Adam was grinning as he hurried over. "Seriously, Brooke. You have to do this show. I'll come and coach you and stuff if you want. It'll be a blast!"

Looking down into her best friend's smiling face, Brooke felt her worries melt away. It was great to see him so excited about doing something together. . . .

"Okay, I'll do it," she blurted out before she could change her mind.

"Really?" He laughed, then lifted one hand for a high five. "Awesome! This is going to be epic."

"Yeah." Brooke smiled too, though anxiety was already creeping back into her mind.

But she did her best not to let it take hold. They weren't entering the Olympics, after all—just a tiny local fun show. And Adam would be right there helping her, just like he'd helped her get Foxy past her nervousness about the new jumps. What was the worst that could happen?

• CHAPTER •
5

"BROOKE! BROOKE!" ETHAN CRIED WHEN
Brooke stepped into the kitchen on Thursday after school.
"Where's Adam?"

"Where's Adam? Where's Adam?" Emma chanted.

"Adam isn't here." Brooke went to the pantry and
grabbed a granola bar. "He has a dentist appointment."

"Oh." Her little brother's face fell. "I wanted to show
him my new cowboy book I got from the lie-berry."

"Li*brary*," Brooke's mother corrected, glancing over
from the counter, where she was fiddling with the coffee
machine.

Brooke unwrapped the granola bar and took a bite.

"Maybe you can show him tomorrow, E," she mumbled through the food in her mouth. "He'll be here then."

Brooke's mother turned and looked Brooke up and down. "Why don't you take off your coat and stay awhile," she said with a smile.

"I was going to run out and check Foxy's water trough," Brooke said, shoving the last of her snack into her mouth. "Be right back."

She headed for the back door, already bracing herself for the cold, which had returned full force, along with some ominous-looking gray storm clouds and a chilly, gusty wind. Hurrying across the backyard, she headed straight for the trough, which was along the fence outside Foxy's shed near the hydrant. There was a thin skin of ice on the top, so Brooke picked up the small hoe leaning against the side of the shed and poked at the ice to break it up. Foxy spotted her from where she'd been standing across the field near the drafts, and came wandering over.

"Hey, girl." Brooke set down her makeshift icebreaker and reached over the fence to scratch the mare's fuzzy neck. "I'm giving you the day off today, but we'll do more jumping tomorrow, okay?"

She'd decided on that plan when Adam had told her about his appointment earlier. There didn't seem to be much point in trying to prepare for the show without him, especially on such a cold day.

"Haley always gives Wings a day off each week," she told Foxy, still scratching her. "Besides, it's pretty chilly today, and I heard tomorrow should be nicer, so—"

"Brooke! Brooke!"

Brooke jumped, startled by the shriek of her little brother. When she looked over her shoulder, both twins were racing across the yard toward her. Emma's jacket was only half-zipped, and Ethan was missing a mitten.

"Wait, you two!" Their mother emerged behind them, pulling on her wool coat with one hand and holding the second mitten in her other. "Ethan, put this on!"

The twins ignored her as they flung themselves at Brooke. "We want to ride again!" Emma cried, throwing her arms around Brooke's waist. "Can we, please, please, please?"

"Yeah. Foxy misses us," Ethan added.

"Sorry," Brooke said, not really feeling sorry at all. "Foxy has the day off today."

Ethan was already reaching between the fence boards to pat Foxy, who had lowered her head toward him. "She doesn't want a day off," he said. "She wants to go for a gallop across the plains."

By then their mother had caught up. "Ethan, mitten on, or no riding," she said firmly.

"Okay." Ethan yanked on his mitten. "Now I'm ready!"

Brooke shot her mother a beseeching look. "Foxy has been working hard lately, Mom," she explained. "I was planning to give her the day off. Maybe we could go over and ask if they could ride the drafts instead?"

She was sure the neighbors would say yes. They were an older couple who both seemed to adore the twins. And they'd always been generous about letting Brooke ride their huge but gentle draft horses, which was how she'd gotten her start riding when she was even younger than Ethan and Emma were now.

Her mother frowned, shooting a look at the drafts snoozing under the tree on the far side of Foxy's pasture. "Listen,

Brooke," she said in a clipped tone. "The kids just want a short ride, so there's no need to start a whole production over it."

"But Foxy—" Brooke began.

"Foxy won't even notice the twins up there," her mother said, cutting her off. "Besides, why on earth are we paying all this money to keep that pony if she can't be used when we need her?"

Brooke opened her mouth to argue, then shut it again without saying anything. She recognized the expression on her mother's face. It said that she'd already made up her mind about this, and nothing Brooke could say was going to change it.

Besides, Brooke couldn't help feeling a little nervous about that last comment. While Brooke spent most of her own money paying for fly spray, grooming stuff, and tack for her pony, her parents covered all the big bills, like feed, vet care, and the farrier who came every other month to trim Foxy's hooves. The last thing Brooke wanted was for her mother to decide they weren't getting their money's worth.

"Okay, fine," she said shortly. "But it's cold, so it'll have to be a short ride."

She got Foxy groomed and tacked up in record time. Emma watched as Brooke untied the lead rope from the fence and started to lead the pony out into the pasture. "Don't forget the bridle," Emma said.

"She's okay in just her halter," Brooke said. "That's what we did last time, remember?"

Ethan had been poking at the water in the trough with a stick, but heard them and ran over. "No, she has to have a bridle," he said. "All good cow ponies wear a bridle." Tossing his stick aside, he dashed for the barn. "I'll get it!"

"Fine, whatever," Brooke muttered, once again deciding it wasn't worth the effort to argue. She could lead Foxy just as easily by the reins of her bridle as with a halter and lead rope. And if it kept the twins happy and made this whole ordeal shorter? Totally worth it.

At first the pony rides went pretty smoothly. Foxy was in a quiet mood and plodded along almost as calmly as the drafts might have. Ethan bounced in the saddle, chattering about being a cowboy, while Emma just sang to herself and clutched the horn as she swayed along.

"Okay, there we go." Finishing Emma's circuit of the

field, Brooke stopped in front of their mother, who was watching from just inside the pasture gate. "All done."

"No, I want to go again!" Ethan cried.

Brooke sighed, shooting a sidelong glance at her mother. "Aren't you two getting cold?" she asked the twins. "We could go in and have some cocoa."

"No! Ride again!" Ethan shouted.

"Just one more turn each," their mother spoke up. "Then back inside to warm up, all right?"

"Yay!" Ethan cheered, rushing over and smacking his twin on the foot. "Get off. It's my turn!"

Soon the twins had switched places. "Okay, hold on," Brooke said. "Here we go."

"Wait!" Ethan said. "I want to ride all by myself this time."

"What do you mean?" Brooke actually glanced over her shoulder to make sure Emma hadn't clambered back into the saddle with her brother while Brooke hadn't been looking. "You are all by yourself."

"No, *all* by myself," he insisted. "Without you leading her."

Brooke gulped. "That's not such a good idea. Foxy's not used to people other than me riding her."

"Yes she is," Ethan insisted. "I ride her all the time!"

Brooke wanted to point out that that wasn't exactly true. Before she could say a word, though, her mother wandered closer.

"Just go ahead and let him try it for a minute," she said. "It'll be fine."

"Okay," Brooke said reluctantly. "But I'll stay right next to you just in case, okay, E?"

He grabbed the reins as she looped them back over the pony's neck. "Okay. Giddyup, Foxy!" he said, thumping her sides with his heels.

The pony lifted her head, a little startled, but stepped off calmly when Brooke let out a soft cluck. "Gently," she told Ethan. "And don't pull too hard on the reins, okay? Um, a real cowboy never does that."

"I know that." He loosened the reins until they were flopping on either side of the pony's neck. "I'm a good rider. Turn left, Foxy!"

He yanked suddenly on the left rein, causing Foxy to

lift her head again and Brooke to hold her breath. But the pony veered off in the direction Ethan wanted, with little more than a confused ear twitch showing her reaction to the little boy's rough aids.

Good girl, Brooke thought, hoping that Foxy could read her mind. *Good, good girl. Don't worry, we're almost finished. . . .*

She glanced up at her brother—just as he lifted both arms, slapped both reins down on Foxy's neck, and kicked hard with both legs at the same time. "Hi-yah!" he yelled. "Let's gallop!"

Foxy jumped in place, startled, and let out a snort of alarm. Brooke stepped forward quickly, grabbing the bridle before the pony could decide to take Ethan's command seriously.

"Easy, girl," she cooed. Then she shot her little brother a stern look. "Don't do that!"

"Why not?" Ethan stuck out his lower lip. "I want to gallop."

"My turn!" Emma yelled, running toward them. "I'm getting cold. Hurry up!"

Foxy was still on alert. At the sound of Emma's shrieks, the pony spun around, and Ethan wobbled in the saddle.

"Hold on to the horn!" Brooke yelped, trying to hang on to the bridle and reach back to steady her brother at the same time.

Luckily her mother finally seemed to notice that things weren't going well. "Everything okay, kids?" she asked, hurrying over.

"I think Foxy's getting upset," Brooke told her.

"No she's not," Ethan argued. "She just wants to gallop."

"Hmm." Their mother eyed the pony. "I think I just felt a drop of rain. That means pony rides are over. Back in the house, you two."

She reached up to drag Ethan out of the saddle, causing him to start yelling and wiggling. Emma was already whining about not getting her second turn, but Mrs. Rhodes ignored her, grabbing the little girl's hand and dragging her off across the yard without a backward glance.

"You're welcome," Brooke muttered as she watched her

family disappear into the nice, warm house. She gave Foxy a pat, and the mare jumped, her ears twitching and her eyes a little wider than usual.

Yikes. She really did seem awfully worked up. Remembering one of the lessons she'd learned at camp—that it was always best to end a ride on a positive note—Brooke decided she'd better hop on and ride for a few minutes to make sure Foxy wasn't too upset by Ethan's cowboying.

It took a couple of tries to mount, since Foxy kept trying to step away. But finally Brooke was in the saddle.

"Easy, girl," she murmured as Foxy shifted beneath her. "You're okay. Let's just walk around a little, okay?"

She nudged the mare with her legs, but instead of stepping off at a walk, Foxy burst into a choppy trot. Brooke gritted her teeth, resisting the urge to yank on the reins. Instead she talked quietly to the pony while using her seat and weight aids to ask Foxy to slow. After a moment Foxy started to respond, slowing to a rapid walk and then a calmer amble.

"Good girl." Brooke smiled, proud of her pony.

Foxy let out a snort, stretching her head forward as

she wandered across the field. Brooke rode for a few more minutes at a walk and a slow trot, before the rain started in earnest and she called it quits.

After dinner Brooke went to her room and logged on to the Pony Post. There were new posts from Nina and Haley, mostly just checking in to see how Maddie was doing. But then Brooke noticed that Haley's entry had been posted just a minute or two earlier.

After opening a new text box, Brooke typed quickly:

[BROOKE] Hi! I'm here too—hi Haley!

Haley responded almost immediately.

[HALEY] Hi! I hope Maddie checks in soon.

[BROOKE] She's prob at the barn spending all the time she can w/ Cloudy. I know that's what I'd be doing if I were in her shoes. Hang in there, Maddie! We will help if we can!!!

[HALEY] Def!!!! Hey, B, did u ride today?

Brooke's fingers hovered over the keys for a moment as she wondered again whether to tell her friends about the show she'd agreed to do. But she decided to wait a little longer. The weather was pretty unpredictable lately. Who knew if the show would even happen? Besides, everyone was still focused on Maddie right now, and Brooke definitely didn't want to distract the others from that.

[BROOKE] Only for a few min. My little sibs

are still on their cowboy kick. They both

followed me out to the barn when I went to

check Foxy's water and pestered me until

I gave them another pony ride. Argh!

[HALEY] Lol, sounds cute! Post more pix, OK?

Anyway, I'd better go—almost time to set the table

for dinner. Check in when u can, Maddie! Bye, B!

[BROOKE] Bye!

She clicked off, still wondering if she should have filled Haley in about her show. But she decided not to worry about it. The show was still more than a week away; there would be plenty of time to tell them once Maddie had figured out what was going on with her family's move.

◆ CHAPTER ◆
6

AFTER THE FINAL BELL ON FRIDAY, BROOKE was on her way to her bus when she spotted Kiersten walking ahead of her. Speeding up, she fell into step with the new girl.

"Hi," she said, still feeling a little shy about just walking up and talking to someone she hardly knew. "How's it going?"

Kiersten smiled. "Fine," she said. "What about you? Any big plans for the weekend?"

"Sort of." Brooke shifted her backpack to her other shoulder. "If the weather doesn't get bad again, I'm hoping to do tons of riding."

"That sounds cool." Kiersten looked a little wistful. "I used to love spending all weekend at the barn too."

Oops. Brooke hadn't meant to make her feel bad. Should she invite Kiersten out to see Foxy, maybe even go for a ride or something?

Then she remembered why she was planning to ride so much, and realized that sort of thing would have to wait. "See, my friend Adam wants me to do this horse show near where I live," Brooke explained. "Um, so I need to really do a lot of riding and jumping and stuff to make sure Foxy and I are ready, you know?"

"A show?" Kiersten sounded interested. "What kind of show? I used to—"

"Brooke!" Adam raced up to them, interrupting the new girl. "Guess what? I entered you in the show online just now in study hall."

"You did?" Brooke felt her stomach flip over with nervousness.

"Uh-huh." Adam looked pleased with himself. "It's official! I mean, I didn't pick out your exact classes or anything, but we can probably do that when we get there."

"Yeah, I'm sure you can," Kiersten put in. "That's usually how shows work."

Adam blinked at her, seeming surprised to see her standing there. "Okay." Shifting his gaze back to Brooke, he grinned. "So let's get home and make sure Foxy's ready to kick butt!"

"Good luck with your schooling. See you Monday, Brooke," Kiersten said, shooting her a quick smile before hurrying off toward her own bus.

As soon as she and Adam walked into the house, Brooke knew they were in trouble. The twins were waiting for them just inside.

"Adam!" Ethan howled, flinging himself forward.

Adam caught him and swung him around. "Yo, little buddy."

Meanwhile Emma tugged on Brooke's sleeve. "We want to go riding," she announced.

Brooke gritted her teeth. As she'd told Kiersten earlier, she and Foxy had a lot of work to do if they didn't want to embarrass themselves at that show. How were they going to get anything done with the twins pestering her for rides every five minutes?

She was about to tell them no way, but Adam responded first. "I can take them for a quick spin if you want," he told Brooke. "You know, while you get changed into your riding clothes."

Brooke's mother appeared just in time to hear him. "Oh, Adam, that would be wonderful!" she exclaimed. "The twins haven't stopped talking about how much they've been enjoying their rides."

"No problem." Adam grinned at Brooke. "Take your time getting changed."

Brooke didn't follow his advice, exchanging her school clothes for her riding jeans and paddock boots in record time. When she was ready, she paused by the window, peering in the direction of the pasture. She couldn't see Foxy or Adam or the twins, though she spotted her mother standing in the middle of the yard bent over her phone.

When she got outside, Adam was on Foxy bareback, with a giggling Emma sitting in front of him. Brooke's mother had made it to the gate to watch by then, and she glanced over as Brooke stopped beside her.

"Adam's so good with the twins," Mrs. Rhodes said with a smile.

Brooke barely heard her mother's words. She was watching Foxy, who looked a little anxious, though only someone who knew her well would notice. In any case, she was behaving herself so far, letting Adam steer her along at a slow walk.

"My turn!" Ethan yelled as Adam rode the pony back toward the gate.

"Okay, hold your horses, dude." Adam laughed. "Get it? Hold your horses?"

Both twins giggled loudly, and Brooke stepped forward to help Adam exchange one twin for the other. As soon as Ethan was in place, he grabbed the reins in front of where Adam was holding them.

"I can steer," he announced. "I know how."

"No!" Brooke blurted, remembering how upset Foxy had been the last time Ethan had tried to "steer" her. "Adam will steer."

Adam glanced down at her and shrugged. "Okay, you heard her, bud," he told Ethan.

"No!" The little boy's face went all stern and stubborn. "Me!"

"Then you can get off right now," Brooke snapped.

"Wait. I have a proposition for you, E," Adam said. "If you let me do the steering, we can try a little trot. How about that? Only real cowboys can trot bareback, you know."

"Okay." Instantly Ethan was all smiles again. "Giddyup, Foxy!"

Adam nudged the pony into a trot. Ethan squealed with glee, which made Foxy speed up a little.

"Careful!" Brooke called. "You're getting pretty close to that—"

She gasped as Adam steered toward one of the crossrails—and Foxy trotted right over it!

"Whee!" Ethan yelled. "Do it again, do it again!"

"No, I want to try!" Emma shrieked, climbing up the fence and waving her arms. "Me, me!"

Brooke watched Foxy, who looked high headed and

a little prancey as Adam turned her and aimed her at the same jump going the opposite way. This time the mare actually broke into a choppy canter a couple of strides out and leaped over with a snort. That made Ethan cheer even louder.

"Okay, that's enough jumping!" Brooke called loudly.

"But I didn't get to do it yet!" Emma complained.

Their mother stepped forward, arms wrapped around herself. She wasn't exactly dressed for the weather, in her stylish but not very warm leather jacket.

"Brooke's right. That's enough for today," she said. "It's freezing out here! Emma, you can try jumping another time. Let's go in and warm up by making some cocoa and cookies, hmm?"

"Cookies!" Emma cried happily. "Since Ethan got to jump, I get to lick the spoon!"

"What? No!" Ethan shouted, practically launching himself from Foxy's back.

Brooke stepped forward just in time to catch him. "Oof," she said, setting him down. "Go on. First one to the house gets the first cup of cocoa."

After her family had disappeared inside, Brooke saddled up and mounted. Foxy felt tense again, and when Brooke asked her to walk, she scooted to the side instead.

"She feels sort of skittish," Brooke told Adam, who was adjusting the jumps.

He glanced over. "Really? She felt fine to me."

Brooke shortened her reins and asked for a walk again. This time Foxy obeyed, though her head stayed high and her steps were short and choppy.

"No, she's definitely a little freaked-out." Brooke steered in a circle, which finally made the pony lower her head a little. "I'd better do plenty of warming up on the flat before we even think about jumping."

"Okay, you're the boss." Adam leaned against the fence and watched as Brooke put the mare through her paces. Foxy settled down quite a bit, though she still seemed ready to burst into a faster gait at any moment.

Finally Adam waved toward the jumps. "Give it a try," he called.

"I'm not sure she's ready yet." Brooke brought Foxy to a

halt, which only lasted a few seconds before Foxy stepped off again without being asked.

"What's the big deal?" Adam shrugged. "You can ride that pony through anything. You guys are an awesome team!"

Brooke couldn't help feeling flattered. Maybe he was right; maybe Brooke was making too big a deal of this. *Borrowing trouble*, as her grandfather liked to say. After all, she'd trained Foxy from the ground up, riding her all over the countryside, through creeks, up and down hills, past scary tractors and cows and flocks of geese, and much more. They'd survived all that just fine. What were a few small jumps?

"Okay. I guess we could try one and see how it goes. . . ." She turned Foxy toward the nearest crossrail and asked her to trot. Foxy surged forward, breaking into a canter just as she'd done on Ethan's second jump.

"Excellent!" Adam cried as the pony landed and raced away. "She looked really good."

"Thanks," Brooke said breathlessly. "She rushed it a little, though."

"That's probably just because she's still new to jumping. Try another one."

After the twins went to bed that evening, Brooke couldn't resist complaining to her mother, who was over at the sink washing up after dinner. "Can't they lay off the riding at least until after my show?" she asked, picking up a dishrag to dry the plate her mother had just washed. "It's getting Foxy all riled up, and I need her to be calm if we're going to be ready to do our best."

Her mother glanced at her with a serene smile. For some reason doing the dishes always helped her relax, which was why she'd always refused her husband's offers to install a dishwasher.

"I know sharing is hard, Brooke," she said.

"It's not that," Brooke protested. "It's just that Foxy is still green. Like, today she kept rushing all our jumps, and I'm pretty sure it's because of the twins riding before."

"Just try to be patient with them, sweetie, hmm?" Brooke's mother handed over another plate. "Think back to how horse crazy you were at that age. What if the

Stockleys had gotten impatient with you pestering them to ride their horses all the time?"

Brooke focused on the plate, not saying anything. She didn't remember those days like that at all. She'd been even shyer back then, and never would have dared pester anyone. It was Mr. Stockley who'd noticed her staring longingly at the drafts, feeding them handfuls of grass whenever they came close enough to the fence. He'd offered to give her a pony ride, and when he and his wife had seen how much she'd loved it, they'd started inviting her over all the time.

But that was all beside the point. Setting the dish down, she shot a sidelong look at her mother. Why had Brooke even bothered to try to talk to her about this?

At least I always have the Pony Post to vent to, Brooke thought, twisting the dishtowel between her hands. *They always understand.*

• CHAPTER •
7

SATURDAY MORNING DAWNED COOL, OVER-
cast, and breezy. Brooke's stepfather had the radio on
during breakfast, and the newscaster predicted scattered
showers all day.

"Uh-oh, better cancel that ten-mile jog I had planned
for today," he joked, buttering a third piece of toast.

Brooke's mother rolled her eyes. "Good. Then you can
help me clean the basement instead."

Brooke shoveled one last bite of cereal into her mouth,
then stood up. "May I be excused?" she asked, shooting
a look at the window. "Adam should be here soon." She
purposely didn't mention riding, not wanting to set off

the twins, who were squabbling over the last blueberry muffin.

"Of course, honey," her mother said.

Brooke hurried upstairs to put on her boots. When she noticed her laptop on the desk, she remembered she hadn't checked in with the Pony Post yet that morning. When she'd logged on the night before, there had been an update from Maddie, though it hadn't said much except that she still hadn't talked to her parents yet about seeing those plane tickets. There was another post from Maddie when Brooke logged on now, though it mostly talked about how her friend Bridget had taken a lesson on Cloudy the afternoon before. Brooke scanned it, then opened her own text box.

[BROOKE] Hi, Maddie. Sorry you didn't get to ride Cloudy again. As you know, I know how you feel! But I'm determined to ride my own pony today if it's the last thing I do, lol. Just hoping the rain holds off. At least it's not cold enough to snow here yet! Did you get the snowstorm you were expecting, Haley?

Nobody else seemed to be on the site just then, so Brooke signed off and went to her closet to grab her paddock boots. When she got downstairs, her stepfather had disappeared, and the twins were in the living room making a mess with their mother's big Rubbermaid tub of wrapping paper.

"Does Mom know you got that stuff out?" Brooke asked, pausing in the doorway.

Her mother hurried in from the kitchen just in time to hear her. "Yes, it's okay," she said. "They have a birthday party to go to tomorrow afternoon, so I told them they could wrap the gift themselves."

"Oh, okay." Brooke was glad to hear that the twins would be busy not only today but tomorrow as well.

The cold and damp wrapped around her as soon as she went outside. Adam hadn't arrived yet, but she decided she'd better not wait for him, in case the weather got even worse, so she quickly tacked up and started her warm-up. Foxy was a little stubborn, first tossing her head when Brooke tried to bridle her and then refusing to leg-yield when asked, even though they'd been practicing the move all fall.

But Brooke did her best to work through the pony's attitude, calmly asking her to walk and trot all around the field. Finally Brooke asked for the leg-yield again, and this time Foxy grudgingly moved sideways a step or two. Deciding that was progress, Brooke halted and gave the pony a pat.

"Where's Adam, anyway?" she muttered, realizing he was late. When she checked her watch, Foxy tossed her head, ripping both reins out of her hands. "Would you quit that?" Brooke exclaimed, quickly gathering them up again. "Stop being so silly."

She asked the pony to trot again and rode her in a big circle. When Brooke brought Foxy back to a walk a few minutes later, she saw Adam letting himself into the pasture.

"Finally!" she exclaimed, riding toward him.

"Sorry I'm late," he said, sounding out of breath. "I got sort of distracted texting with the guys from the team."

"The basketball team?" Brooke was surprised. Adam had barely mentioned any of his guy friends all week, especially the ones who'd made the team.

Adam didn't answer, stepping over to pat Foxy on the neck. "Looks like she's all warmed up," he said. "Ready to start jumping?"

Feeling a cold splash on her arm, Brooke squinted up at the clouds. "I think it's starting to rain."

"Just a little." Adam headed toward the jumps. "Come on. I'll set up two in a row . . ."

Ignoring the sporadic drizzle, they got to work. Adam turned out to be a good coach, and Foxy finally settled down and behaved like her usual agreeable self. By the time the rain started coming down more steadily, Brooke was feeling pretty good about things.

She led Foxy into the pony part of the barn to untack. "I hope the twins are done with riding," she told Adam as he unbuckled one side of the girth. "At least until after the show."

"Why?" Adam dragged the saddle off the pony's back. "They're pretty cute about the whole cowboy thing."

"Yeah, but I think letting them ride is having a negative effect on Foxy," Brooke said as she clipped Foxy's halter back on. "I mean, she's still young and pretty green. I could definitely tell the difference between yesterday and today."

Adam shrugged, setting the saddle onto the half door leading into the people part of the barn. "She'll be okay," he said. "She's a superstar, remember?"

"Yeah." Brooke smiled and patted the pony, deciding that maybe Adam was right. Maybe she was just borrowing trouble.

Sunday was Maddie's birthday, and Brooke made sure to post a Happy Birthday message first thing when she got up. She was surprised to see that Haley had actually beaten her to it, even though it was an hour earlier in Wisconsin. Then again, maybe that wasn't such a surprise. Haley and her family lived on a working farm, with not only horses but cows and chickens as well. She always got up early, even on the weekends.

I hope Maddie's party goes okay this afternoon, Brooke thought as she pulled on her clothes and brushed her teeth. Over the past couple of days, Maddie had told the other Pony Posters that she wanted to wait until after her birthday to talk to her parents about the move. But it already sounded to Brooke as if Maddie was starting to accept that it was definitely going to happen.

Thinking about that made Brooke feel sad. Maddie had such a special connection with Cloudy, but the pony didn't belong to her. There was no way Cloudy would be going with the family when they moved. How would Maddie ever recover from losing such an amazing pony?

Brooke shook her head, deciding not to think such depressing thoughts, at least right now. The whole Pony Post would be there to support Maddie through whatever happened. For the moment, though, all Brooke could do was wait for her friend's next update.

Adam couldn't make it over until after lunch, since his family went to church on Sunday mornings, so after breakfast Brooke did all her homework for the weekend. She was halfway through her word problems for math when her mother stuck her head into the room to let Brooke know they were leaving for the twins' friend's party.

"We'll be back around two or three," she said, looking oddly informal in jeans and a cardigan.

"Okay." Brooke wandered to the window and watched as her stepfather helped the twins into the SUV and then shoved a huge, sloppily wrapped gift in beside them. Then Brooke texted Adam, reminding him to get there as soon as he could. With any luck they'd be able to finish their ride before her family got home.

An hour later she glanced at the clock after finishing the last of her homework, and realized that Adam would be there in less than fifteen minutes. After logging on to the Pony Post, she quickly typed in another brief message for Maddie, wishing her well at the party. Then Brooke hurried downstairs, gulped down half a sandwich, and headed out to the barn.

It was still cold, but the clouds had cleared out and the wind was barely a whisper. While she tacked up, Brooke went back to brooding over Maddie's problem. It was weird to think of her living in a whole other country, though it really wouldn't affect Maddie's friendship with the other Pony Posters much, other than adjusting to an even bigger time difference. Her friendship with Cloudy? That was another matter. . . .

"Hey, there you are!" Adam exclaimed, hurrying into view around the corner of the shed. "I knocked at the house but nobody answered."

"Everyone's out at some kiddie party." Brooke tightened the girth another notch. "So we should have some peace and quiet for a change."

"Cool." Adam handed her the bridle, which she'd hung on the door. "So, what are we waiting for?"

Brooke quickly bridled her pony and led her out to the stump she used as a mounting block. *I shouldn't take this for granted,* she thought, her mind still mostly on Maddie. *No matter how annoying it is to have to share Foxy with the twins, at least I know I won't have to move and leave her behind—*

"Watch it!" Adam warned as Foxy lifted her head and sidestepped just as Brooke was putting her foot into the stirrup. "Here, I'll hold her while you get on."

"Thanks." Brooke swung aboard quickly, though the pony moved forward, bumping into Adam, before Brooke could get her right foot into the stirrup. "Whoa, Foxy! Hold still."

"It's okay. She's just excited about doing more jumping. Right, Foxy girl?" Adam rubbed the mare's face.

Brooke shoved her foot into the stirrup and shortened her reins. "We need to warm up before we start jumping," she reminded Adam.

"Okay, so do it." He grinned at her, stepping back out of the way.

Brooke's mind wandered back to Maddie as she aimed Foxy out into the field and asked her to trot. She got into two-point position, letting the mare stretch out.

She was trying to picture Maddie wandering the streets of London, when a sudden gust of wind blew some dry leaves up in front of them. Foxy snorted, slammed on the brakes, and spun around.

"Whoa!" Brooke cried, grabbing a handful of mane and barely staying in the saddle. She'd lost both her stirrups, but quickly jammed her feet back in. "Stop that, Foxy!"

"You okay?" Adam called from over by the gate. "What happened?"

"I don't know." Brooke frowned, a little annoyed with

the mare, who rarely spooked at anything. Why had a few blowing leaves set her off?

Because I wasn't paying attention, she realized. *Better forget about Maddie for now and focus on my ride, or I'll end up on the ground next time.*

"Okay, Foxy," she said, giving the mare a firm nudge with both heels. "Walk on, and let's get down to business."

Half an hour later Brooke was in a much better mood. Foxy's silliness had passed, and she was working like a pro, doing basic dressage moves and hopping over the jumps as if they were nothing. For the first time Brooke found herself actually looking forward to the show.

She brought the pony to a square halt after a line of two jumps. "Good girl," she said, giving her a pat. "You know, maybe it'll be kind of fun to show you off to everyone next weekend."

She glanced at Adam, not sure if he was close enough to hear what she'd said. But he wasn't even looking at her. He was peering in the direction of the driveway.

"Look out—incoming," he said.

"Huh?" At first Brooke wasn't sure what he was talking

about. Then she heard the slam of a car door from that direction, and a second later Ethan came barreling across the backyard, with Emma a few steps behind him.

"Hi, Foxy!" Ethan shouted. "Want to go for a ride?"

"Stop!" Brooke's mother hollered, running after the twins. She grabbed them each by an arm as they started to duck between the fence boards. "No playing with the pony in your party clothes."

"Aw, Mommy!" Emma whined.

But Ethan didn't look that upset. "It's okay," he told his twin. "We'll be able to ride her a lot at the party next week."

"Huh?" Brooke frowned at him, wondering if she'd heard him wrong. "What do you mean? What party?"

Ethan grinned up at her. "Owen is having a birthday party on Saturday," he said. "He has a huge yard, bigger than Foxy's whole pasture even! So I told him we'd bring Foxy and everyone could go for pony rides."

"With lots of galloping and jumping," Emma added cheerfully.

"What?" Brooke yelped. "No way!"

By then her stepfather had strolled over to join them. He chuckled and tousled Ethan's hair. "Don't worry, Brookie," he said with a wink. "I imagine they'll forget all about it by next Saturday."

"No I won't!" Ethan wiggled away and glared up at him. "I *promised* Owen I'd bring her!"

"Too bad," Brooke snapped. "Because Foxy's going to a horse show next Saturday, not your dumb party."

"Yeah, we can't miss the show," Adam put in.

"Settle down, Brooke. There's no need to get worked up. I'll speak to the child's mother and deal with whatever promises Ethan made," Brooke's mother said, rolling her eyes. "Now come on, you two—let's get you inside and changed before you make yourselves filthy."

That night Adam stayed for dinner—just like old times—and then hung around to play board games with the whole family. Brooke was having so much fun that she actually forgot about the Pony Post for a while. But when she went upstairs to take a bath, she suddenly remembered, grabbed her laptop, and logged on right away.

She scrolled past a couple of posts by Haley and Nina until she reached one from Maddie. Brooke's heart leaped as she read it.

[MADDIE] I'm back! Thanx for the extra b'day wishes! The party was super-fun. About a zillion people came, and I think everyone had a good time. But I'll tell u more about that later. First I have some AMAZING news: WE'RE NOT MOVING!!!!

Brooke gasped, eagerly scanning the rest of the post. Maddie explained that it had all been a big misunderstanding. Yes, her parents had reserved plane tickets to London for the whole family. But they were for a fun vacation, not a move.

"Wow," Brooke whispered. "A trip to England? Cool!"

Below that news was another post from Maddie. Brooke was surprised to see her own name near the beginning.

[MADDIE] Btw, Brooke, I hope your lil bro and
sis are letting you ride Foxy again by now. B/c I
def. know how you feel about having to share.
I mean, I'm used to having to share Cloudy
with other lesson students and stuff. But it
was still rough being expected to share MY
Cloudy with someone else all the time—even
tho that someone else is one of my bffs!!

Brooke smiled, amazed as always by the way her Pony
Post friends seemed to really get her. She opened a text
box and started to type.

[BROOKE] YAY MADDIE! I'm so glad you don't
have to leave Cloudy behind! What a great
birthday gift. As for the twins, they haven't ridden
F. since Fri, and I'm glad about that. I'm afraid
having them ride is confusing Foxy and hurting
her training, and I don't want that to happen, esp.
now. See, I've been meaning to tell u all—Adam
talked me into entering a horse show next Sat. It's

riding distance from here and he says it's mostly for green horses and riders, so he thinks we'll do great. But I'm not so sure if E&E keep messing up Foxy's training . . . But whatevs, we had two good rides this w/e, so maybe we'll do OK after all!

She yawned as she hit enter. It was tempting to wait around to see if any of the other Pony Posters checked in soon, but it had been a long, busy weekend, and she wasn't sure she could keep her eyes open that long. She logged off and went to take her bath.

✦ CHAPTER ✦

8

"TRY IT AGAIN," ADAM SAID AS BROOKE trotted past him after jumping a crossrail. Well, not *jumping* it exactly. . . .

"I think she's getting bored with hopping over the same three jumps all the time," Brooke said, bringing the pony to a halt. "That's probably why she's started just trotting over the crossrails instead of actually jumping them."

"Hmm." Adam scratched his chin, glancing around at their homemade jumps. "She doesn't do that with the coop, though."

Brooke shrugged. "That's because it's taller."

"Oh!" He grinned. "Okay, then we have our solution."

He hurried toward the nearest crossrail and lifted the pole out of the notch.

"What are you doing?" Brooke asked.

"Making it higher," he replied, sliding the rail farther up the standard. "Then she'll start jumping again, right?"

"I guess." Brooke felt a shiver of nerves as she watched him set the jump at the new height. Still, she reminded herself that even at the higher height the jump was lower than the ones they'd done at camp. "No problem. Right, Foxy?" she murmured, giving the pony a pat.

As Adam adjusted the second jump, there was a yell from the back door. It was the twins. Both of them were dressed in jeans and puffy jackets.

"Hey, Brooke!" Ethan hollered as he ran toward her. "Mom said we can ride, since we didn't get to yesterday."

"What?" Brooke looked toward the house just in time to see her mother emerge, looking frazzled as she zipped up her down jacket with the hand not clutching her cell phone.

"You don't mind, do you, Brooke?" she called, waving the phone as she came toward the pasture. "I really need to check my messages, and they won't give me a moment's peace."

Brooke frowned, wanting to say no but not quite daring—not with her mother looking like she was ready to blow her top. "Um, sure," Brooke said. "But we have to keep it short, okay? We're sort of in the middle of something."

"Yeah," Adam said. "But hey, Foxy could probably use a break."

"Thanks, kids." Looking relieved, Mrs. Rhodes patted Emma on the head. "Be good, you two," she said, then wandered over to lean against the barn as she pressed the phone to her ear.

As Brooke dismounted, Ethan stared at Foxy. "Hey, that's not my cowboy saddle," he said.

Brooke glanced at her English saddle. "We don't have time to change saddles."

"Yeah," Adam said quickly as the little boy's frown deepened. "But that's okay, because this is a super-special mega-cowboy saddle. Only the greatest bronc riders use them."

"Really?" Ethan looked slightly suspicious, but he

didn't argue as Adam swung him into the saddle and adjusted the stirrups.

Brooke rushed her brother through his pony ride, circling half the pasture instead of all of it and urging Foxy into a trot at the end just to get back sooner. "Okay, next rider up!" she called, waving Emma forward.

"I want Adam to lead me," Emma said. "Not you, Brooke. You're too bossy."

Brooke couldn't help snorting and rolling her eyes at that. "Look who's talking!"

Adam chuckled and grabbed Emma, tickling her and making her giggle before hoisting her onto Foxy's back. "It's okay. I'll do it," he told Brooke. "Come on, Ems." Taking the reins, he started forward.

Brooke stepped back and watched them go, feeling impatient and rather grumpy. Why did the twins have to come along just when she and Foxy had been making such good progress on their jumping? Still, there wasn't much Brooke could do except hope they didn't demand more than one turn today.

Adam seemed to take forever to lead Foxy and Emma

around the field. Finally he started back across toward where Brooke and Ethan were waiting. Their mother had finished with her phone by then and wandered in to watch.

"Thanks for letting them ride again," she said. "They're really enjoying— Oh dear!"

Adam had clucked Foxy into a trot, just as Brooke had done a few minutes earlier. This time, though, Foxy didn't step into a slow jog like before. Instead she shook her head and leaped forward, ears flattened back. Brooke gasped, realizing that the pony was about to take off at top speed.

Emma shrieked as she started to tip off to the side. Adam yanked on the reins, stopping Foxy in her tracks— and somehow he managed to reach back and steady Emma at the same time.

"Nothing to see here, folks," he called once the pony was still, though his voice sounded a little shaky. "We're okay."

"No I'm not!" Emma yelled, her face beet red. "Foxy tried to make me fall off!"

"Yeah, that was cool!" Ethan ran toward the pony. "Foxy's a bucking bronco! Can I try?"

"No, not right now," his mother said firmly, hurrying

over and lifting Emma out of the saddle, and giving her a big hug before setting her down. "I think that's enough riding for today, you two."

Ethan looked disappointed, but he didn't argue as he patted Foxy on the shoulder. "Make sure you do that at Owen's party, okay, Foxy?" he said with a giggle.

"I already told you, she's *not* going to your friend's party," Brooke snapped, her heart still racing from the close call. "She's going to a horse show with me."

"But I told everyone she was coming!" Ethan protested. "Owen's expecting her!"

"All right, that's enough." Brooke's mother grabbed his hand. "I'll deal with it, Brooke," she said over her shoulder as she dragged the protesting twins toward the house.

"Wow, I wonder what got into Foxy just now," Adam said when they were gone. "I've never seen her like that."

"I told you, the twins get her too revved up." Brooke frowned at him. "She's not used to that sort of thing."

He shrugged and grinned. "Well, at least Ethan got a real cowboy moment out of the deal," he said. "Come on. Let's get back to work."

◆ ◆ ◆

After dinner the twins grabbed the TV remote, insisting on watching some dumb animated movie before bedtime. Not in the mood for family time, Brooke headed upstairs to check the Pony Post. There were a couple of new messages.

[MADDIE] Went to the barn today after school. Aaah, it still feels so good not to have to worry about moving away! Cloudy and I had a great ride. What'd you guys do with yr ponies today?

[HALEY] Wings gets Mondays off, remember? But I gave him a good grooming—he's a total fuzzball! I'll try to get pix soon. Hoping we can go out on our XC course tmw if the ground isn't too hard.

As usual Brooke loved hearing about what her friends were doing with their ponies. It all sounded so exciting! Thanks to her friends' descriptions and photos, she could practically feel as if she was riding along with them sometimes—leaping over huge cross-country fences with

Haley and Wings, ambling along beneath the Spanish moss in some New Orleans park with Nina and Breezy, or exploring the rolling hills of Northern California with Maddie and Cloudy.

Did the others feel the same way about her posts? Brooke wasn't sure. Somehow, riding around the local countryside on Foxy seemed kind of ordinary compared to what the others did. But maybe that was just because she was used to it.

In any case, she couldn't resist sharing, even if today's news wasn't all that great.

[BROOKE] I rode Foxy again today, but the twins came along and interrupted just when she was doing super well. Grr! Anyway, I got back on after, but it wasn't the same. She was all skittish and distracted, looking for monsters everywhere and not paying much attention to me at all. Double grrr! Adam coached me thru it and things got better after a while. We even jumped some higher stuff at the end, and that went pretty well. But it would be nice if I didn't have to go back to square one every time my little

sibs get on and freak her out, u know? Esp. with

this show coming up so soon! Triple grrrrrrrrrr!

She sat back after hitting send, already feeling better for having poured out her day to her friends.

She was about to log off when a new message popped up right below hers.

[NINA] B! Hey, you still on?

Brooke smiled and pulled the laptop closer, typing fast.

[BROOKE] Hi Nina! I'm still here.

[NINA] Yay! Just read your post. Bummer about the twins, huh? But it sounds like you're working thru all Foxy's reactions & stuff.

[BROOKE] I guess. Just wish I didn't have to.

[NINA] I hear u! But that's ponies for u, right? U should have seen me one time when some jerk decided to beep his horn right when I was riding Breezy down the trail by the street! He jumped straight into the air and I was lucky to still be on him when he came down, LOL!

[BROOKE] I can't even imagine riding in the middle of the city like u do! I can barely manage out here in the boonies, lol.

[NINA] Ha! I bet u would do just fine. U and Foxy have a connection, and that's important. She trusts u, right?

[BROOKE] Yah, true. I think that's the only reason she's not freaking out more over the twins' cowboy rides!!!

[NINA] Well, you trained her super well, don't forget that. I know u will do great at that show, no matter how many times your

lil sibs decide to ride between now & then.

And hey, if u start to get nervous, try what

I used to do when I got stage fright before

my dance recitals—just breathe deeply and

count backward from ten a few times.

[BROOKE] Does that rly work?

[NINA] Lol, I guess so! At least I never got that

nervous after I started doing it. Worth a try?

[BROOKE] Def! Thanks Nina!

[NINA] Anytime! Gtg, but make sure

to keep us posted on the show!

[BROOKE] Promise. Nighty-night!

Brooke signed off, still smiling at Nina's pep talk.

Maybe Nina was right. Brooke and Foxy had been

through a lot together over the past few years. Their bond had to be strong enough to get them through the twins' sudden interest in riding too—and through that show with flying colors!

• CHAPTER •

9

ON WEDNESDAY, BROOKE WAS DEEP IN thought as she emerged from the lunch line with her tray of chicken fingers. The show was only three days away now, and she was growing more nervous by the hour. Luckily, the twins hadn't come home from their play date yesterday until it was almost dark, so she'd had Foxy all to herself. Foxy had been a little spooky at the beginning of the ride, but with Adam's encouragement Brooke had ridden her through that and the pony had settled quickly.

"Oops," Brooke blurted out, stopping short just in time to avoid running into Kiersten, who was standing looking around the crowded cafeteria.

The new girl shot Brooke a brief smile. "Sorry," she said, stepping aside.

"It's okay. I wasn't paying attention." Brooke suddenly felt shy. "Um, do you need somewhere to sit? I mean, if you want—my friends and I are right over there. You know—it would be cool if you wanted to sit with us."

She pointed to the girls she usually sat with. Kiersten smiled shyly.

"Sure, if you don't mind," she said. "I mean, that would be great."

The other girls were discussing the latest social studies assignment when Brooke and Kiersten sat down. "Hey, guys," Brooke said. "You all know Kiersten, right?"

"Sure, hi." Her friend Jana sounded distracted as she shot Kiersten a quick but sincere smile. The other two girls added their own greetings. Then they all went back to their conversation.

Brooke wasn't particularly interested in talking about social studies, so she glanced at Kiersten as she opened her milk carton. "So I've been meaning to ask," she said. "You said you used to ride. What kind of riding did you do? Like, English or Western, or what?"

"Actually, I was a jockey at the racetrack," the new girl said. As Brooke's eyes widened, Kiersten giggled. "Kidding! I rode English. Hunter jumper stuff, mostly, plus a little dressage."

"Cool." Brooke picked up a chicken finger and took a bite. "So did you ever do shows?"

"Uh-huh. My whole barn showed pretty often, mostly the local circuit up there in PA."

"Wow. So did you have your own pony?"

"Yeah." Kiersten's face went gloomy. "We had to sell him when my parents got divorced, though."

"Oh! Sorry." Brooke blushed, feeling bad for bringing up a sad subject.

Kiersten glanced at her with a small smile. "It's okay. My trainer found him a really good home, and I'm friends with his new owner on Facebook so I can still see pictures of him, so it all worked out. Sort of." She sighed. "Anyway, that's why we moved here—my mom and me, that is. She wanted to be near her family after my dad left, and well, I didn't get a vote."

"Sorry," Brooke said again. "So are you going to get another pony?"

"Doubtful." Kiersten poked at her green beans. "Mom can't afford it right now, since she's in school to be a nurse and only working part-time. I'll be lucky if I can scrape up enough to take a lesson now and then."

"You don't have to," Brooke said impulsively. "You can come ride Foxy anytime you want."

"Really?" Kiersten's face lit up. "Oh wow, that's so nice of you, Brooke!"

"Anytime after this Saturday, that is," Brooke added hastily. She smiled. "That's when our show is. Remember? The one Adam was talking about the other day?"

"Oh, right." Kiersten nodded. "That's so exciting that you're doing a show! Where is it? Maybe I'll come by and cheer you and Foxy on."

"Sure, that would be great," Brooke said, though a shiver of anxiety ran through her at the thought of it. She was going to be nervous enough as it was without a bunch of people she knew watching!

Kiersten squinted at her. "What's wrong?" she asked.

Then she laughed. "Wait, no, don't tell me—show nerves?"

"Show nerves?" Brooke echoed. "Is that a thing?"

"Totally! I used to get them every time I showed. Don't worry, it gets better. It just takes a few shows to get used to the nerves so you can, like, channel them into positive energy or whatever." Kiersten shrugged and grinned. "That's what my trainer used to call it, anyway. And I guess it worked, because after a while I hardly got nervous anymore."

"Oh, okay." Brooke couldn't imagine not being nervous before something as stressful as a show. But she hoped Kiersten was right. In any case, just knowing that getting nervous was normal made her feel a little less anxious about the coming show.

"So did you decide which divisions to enter yet?" Kiersten asked, reaching for her milk.

"Not yet. We're just sort of working on everything right now." Brooke thought back again to yesterday's ride. "If Adam had his way, we'd spend all day, every day jumping."

Kiersten giggled. "Typical boy!"

"Yeah." Brooke smiled. "Anyway, my friend Haley is

an eventer, and she has her pony on a schedule where they only jump once or twice a week. She says it's better for him mentally and physically. So yesterday I convinced Adam that we should just do flatwork."

"Sounds good. Who's Haley? Does she go here?" Kiersten glanced around the crowded cafeteria.

"Um, no." Brooke felt sheepish, not quite ready to explain her "imaginary friends" to the new girl yet. "She lives pretty far away."

"Oh." Kiersten poked at her chicken. "Well, if you need me to help you get ready for the show or anything, I'd be happy to do it."

"That's okay. Adam will be helping me." Kiersten's face fell, and Brooke quickly added, "But I'd love it if you came to the show on Saturday to watch. You can meet Foxy then too."

"Cool." Kiersten looked happy again. "It's a plan."

More storm clouds rolled in that afternoon, and Brooke had only been riding Foxy for twenty minutes when it started to rain. "Bummer," Adam said as they dashed for the shed. "We didn't even get to start jumping!"

"That's okay." Brooke patted the pony, then reached up to unbuckle her bridle. "Foxy did great, and she could probably use another day off from jumping since we'll be doing a lot of it for the next few days."

"Okay." Adam pulled out his cell phone to check the time. "You okay putting her away and stuff? I should go."

"Sure. See you tomorrow, right?" Brooke pulled off the bridle and hung it over the half door leading into the people part of the barn. "Are you going to take the bus home with me again?"

"I can't," Adam said. "I have something to do right after school. But I'll get someone to drop me off as soon as I'm done."

Brooke was a little surprised; until now, Adam had been talking as if he planned to spend every spare moment helping her train for the show. "Try to get here as soon as you can, okay?" she said. "We have a lot to do if we're going to be ready for Saturday!"

"No worries." Adam gave Foxy a pat. "See you."

As soon as she had the pony settled in for the evening,

Brooke dashed for the house, cringing at the cold rain pelting her face. Inside, the twins were busy with their toys and barely looked up as she hurried toward the stairs.

In her room Brooke changed out of her damp, dirty clothes and then flopped onto her bed with her laptop. She'd just realized she hadn't told the Pony Post about Kiersten yet. After scanning the latest news about her friends and their ponies, she started typing.

[BROOKE] Hi guys! Sounds like you're all having fun with your ponies! Foxy and I had a good ride today, tho it was a short one b/c it started raining. Oh well! The forecast is clear for the rest of the week, which is good. I can't believe the show is so soon!

But never mind that—I forgot to tell u there's a new girl in my class, and guess what? She's a rider! Well, she used to ride, anyway. She had to stop when she moved b/c her parents split up. But I invited her to ride Foxy sometime, and she's coming to watch us at the show. Isn't that cool?

I mean, u guys are great!!! But it's kind of nice

having a horse friend I can talk to f2f too, u know?

She posted her message and then waited a few seconds, but there was no immediate response, so she logged off. Before shutting down her computer, she sent Adam a quick e-mail, reminding him again to come over as soon as he could the next day.

On Thursday afternoon Brooke changed into her riding clothes in record time. She'd sat with Kiersten again that day at lunch, and talking about the show had made her realize how close it was—just two days away now!

"I hope Adam gets here soon," she muttered as she tightened the pony's girth and led her out of the shed. "Come on, Foxy. Let's warm up while we're waiting for him."

She mounted and got to work, asking Foxy to walk, trot, and canter and also practicing some of their other moves, like leg-yields and backing up. It was a relatively warm, pleasant day, and Foxy felt fresh and alert, pricking her ears at blowing leaves and skittering to the side when one of the drafts let out a loud snort on the far side of the fence.

Finally, though, Foxy felt focused and ready to jump. But where was Adam?

Brooke halted near the gate and checked her watch. It had been more than an hour and a half since school had let out. What could be keeping him?

She chewed her lower lip, trying to decide what to do. She definitely didn't want to jump without him there. She and Foxy were still getting back into the swing of things over fences, and even though her mother was right inside, Brooke felt a little nervous about jumping alone.

Besides, Adam was supposed to be coaching her. Wasn't that the whole point of doing this show? Brooke wished she had a cell phone to call or text him with, but every time she asked about getting one, her stepfather kept saying she could have one for her next birthday. In the meantime she had to borrow a phone from one of her parents when she needed one.

"Adam'll probably be here soon," she muttered, tightening her grip on the reins as Foxy shifted impatiently under her. "Come on, girl. Let's do one more trot around the pasture."

When they had finished that, there was still no sign of Adam. Glancing up, Brooke saw that the sky was already going orange and pink with the rapidly approaching sunset. If she wanted to do any jumping today, she couldn't wait much longer.

"Aargh," she said aloud. "I just wish he'd get here already!"

She turned Foxy back across the field, vaguely planning to do some figure eights or something. But she was still watching the sliver of driveway she could see from here, hoping for a glimpse of Adam's bike. As Brooke kicked Foxy into a trot, the pony spooked at something— Brooke wasn't even sure what.

"Hey," Brooke said, pulling her to a halt. "Stop that, Foxy."

The pony snorted and tossed her head. Brooke felt a quiver of nerves but told herself not to freak out. Foxy was just testing her to see if she was paying attention, and she'd flunked the test.

"Sorry, girl," she murmured, giving Foxy a pat and then asking again for the trot.

Ten minutes later she was practicing circles and figure eights when she noticed her mother hurrying across the yard. Brooke rode over, hoping her mother wasn't coming to say that the twins wanted to ride again.

"Brooke," Mrs. Rhodes said. "Adam just called. He asked me to tell you he can't make it over today after all."

"What?" Brooke's heart sank. "Why?"

Her mother shrugged. "I was on the other line, so we didn't get into it."

"Oh. Um, okay, thanks." Brooke shot a look at the jumps as her mother disappeared back into the house. It was tempting to skip jumping for today, wait until tomorrow when Adam could be there to coach her.

But no. Tomorrow was Friday, just one day before the show. If she wanted to be ready, they needed to practice jumping *today*.

Squaring her shoulders, she gathered up her reins. "Come on, Foxy," she said. "We can do this."

She gave the pony a kick, turning her toward the nearest

jump. But Foxy hesitated, flicking her ears back and forth and stepping to the side instead of trotting forward.

"Please, Foxy!" Brooke exclaimed, her determination already seeping away into the mass of nervousness in her gut. "Just let's get through this, okay?"

She kicked again, and the pony spurted forward, half-trotting and half-cantering. Brooke hauled back on the reins, not wanting to rush the jump. Foxy skidded to a halt, tossing her head.

"Quit it!" Brooke cried, suddenly near tears.

Foxy snorted and tossed her head again, prancing to the side. Fed up with the pony's silliness, Brooke gave her a stout kick—and Foxy responded by humping her back and bucking!

Brooke gasped. "Hey!" she blurted out, freezing in shock. Foxy had never bucked under saddle before!

Before Brooke could figure out what to do, Foxy leaped forward, yanking her head down and bucking again—and before Brooke quite knew what was happening, she hit the hard ground with a loud "Oof!"

◆ CHAPTER ◆
10

BROOKE CLIMBED TO HER FEET, SHAKING
all over. She took a few deep breaths, trying to calm her
racing heart. She'd landed on her hip and was pretty sure
she'd have a bruise there by morning, but otherwise she
wasn't hurt. Her glasses had even stayed on, though they
were slightly askew.

Foxy had cantered off a few strides and then stopped,
lowering her head to sniff at the frostbitten grass. As the
pony started to graze, Brooke adjusted her glasses, then
headed toward the pony on trembling legs and grabbed
the dangling reins.

"What was that all about?" she said, her voice as wobbly as the rest of her.

Foxy lifted her head and nudged at her, nickering as if to ask why she was on the ground all of a sudden. Brooke wasn't sure how to react. This wasn't the first time she'd fallen off a horse, of course. The first time had been so long ago that she couldn't even remember it. It wasn't even the first time she'd come off Foxy.

But it's the first time she dumped me on purpose, Brooke thought.

Her eyes filled with tears again. What had happened, anyway? Yes, Foxy had been a little unpredictable lately. But nothing like this!

If Adam had showed up like he was supposed to, it wouldn't have happened, she thought with a sudden flash of resentment. *And if Ethan and Emma didn't keep wanting to play cowboy . . .*

She sighed without bothering to finish the thought, reaching up to give Foxy a rub on the nose. This wasn't Adam's fault. It wasn't really Foxy's, either, or even the twins'. It was just one of those things that happened some-times, especially with a young horse. The best thing to do was get back on and forget about it.

Brooke wasn't sure she could do that, though. At least not right now. She still felt pretty shaky, and that was liable to set Foxy off again. Maybe it would be safer to put her away and try again tomorrow. . . .

Ten minutes later Brooke was back in her room unlacing her paddock boots and wondering if she'd done the right thing. If Adam had been there, he prob-ably could have talked her into getting back on right away. Or even if he couldn't have, he would have been willing to get on himself, ride Foxy around a little so she could end on a good note. A little bucking wouldn't scare him at all.

But it scared me, she admitted, kicking her left boot in the direction of her closet.

She was sure she'd be over it by tomorrow—at least enough to get on and ride again. Nothing could keep her away from Foxy for long.

But that show was another thing entirely. Suddenly it just seemed way too soon, way too much. Luckily, she knew the perfect place to get some advice about what to do.

Soon she was on the Pony Post typing away. She poured out the whole story to her friends, from talking to Kiersten again at lunch to getting bucked off just now. Nobody responded, so she set down the laptop and headed to her parents' room to use the phone.

Adam didn't answer his cell, so she left a message asking him to call her back as soon as he could. Then she wandered back to her room.

She spent the next half hour or so trying to focus on her homework, though she didn't get much done. Finally she gave up and grabbed her laptop again.

There were already a couple of responses to her post.

[NINA] O, B! Naughty Foxy!!! So sorry to hear u came off! Just remember it happens to the best of us.

[HALEY] Ya, when I first started jumping, I

spent more time flying thru the air than in the

saddle, lol. I hope you're not too sore tmw.

Wondering if either of her friends were still on the site, Brooke quickly opened a text box.

[BROOKE] Thanks, guys.

She waited, but no more messages appeared, and she sighed, realizing that Nina and Haley must have already logged off. Too bad; she really could have used someone to talk to right now—someone who understood what she was going through. She wondered if she should try calling Kiersten, but Brooke quickly remembered that she didn't have Kiersten's phone number.

Realizing that Adam hadn't called back yet, she hurried to her parents' room to try again. This time he picked up on the third ring.

"Yo," he said. "Sorry, I was just about to call you back."

"Okay." She took a deep breath. "Um, so what happened to you today? Foxy and I waited for you."

There was a pause. "Uh, actually the coach invited me to basketball practice today."

Why? You're not on the team, Brooke thought, though she stopped herself from saying it.

"Yeah?" she said instead.

"Yeah. You know that kid Victor Robertson?"

Brooke didn't, not really, though she vaguely recognized the name as belonging to a tall kid in the grade ahead of them. "Sort of."

"He broke his leg in two places doing BMX yesterday." Adam sounded excited. "That means he's off the team, obviously, at least for this season. So Coach made me the new alternate!"

Brooke wasn't quite sure how to react to that. "Oh. Um, congratulations?"

"Thanks. But listen, that means I can't make it to your show after all," Adam continued quickly. "Sorry. But we've got an important practice on Saturday, and obviously I have to be there."

"Obviously." Brooke tried not to sound sarcastic, though she didn't quite succeed.

Adam didn't seem to notice. He babbled on for a couple more minutes about his new team uniform and some upcoming game, then said good-bye and hung up, leaving Brooke standing there with the phone in her hand and no idea what to do now.

That night at dinner Brooke couldn't do more than pick at her fish. Luckily, her parents didn't notice, since the twins wouldn't stop talking about the birthday party they were invited to on Saturday.

"And Owen has a pool with a slide!" Ethan said excitedly for about the fifth time. "And *two* diving boards!"

"Just remember, it's way too cold to swim these days," Brooke's mother said, spearing another forkful of creamed spinach. "But maybe Owen will have another party next summer, hmm?"

"We won't have time to swim anyway," Emma put in. "We'll be too busy riding Foxy."

That got Brooke's attention. She couldn't believe the twins still thought they were taking her pony to some random kiddie party! Especially after her bucking fit. Not that Brooke had told her parents about that—she was afraid that if they knew, they'd forbid her from taking the pony to the show that weekend.

Then again, Brooke wasn't even sure she wanted to go anymore. She'd been brooding about it nonstop, trying to figure out what to do. At first she'd assumed that Adam backing out meant she was out too.

But then she'd remembered that he'd already signed her up. Besides, she'd told the other Pony Posters about it, and Kiersten was planning to come watch her ride. . . .

It all just seemed too complicated. Maybe she should tell the twins to go ahead and take Foxy to that party; then she wouldn't have any choice but to back out of the show.

But her mother was already pointing her fork at each twin in turn. "That's enough about the pony rides," she said sternly. "I explained this to you two earlier, remember? Foxy is Brooke's pony, and she's nice enough to share her with you sometimes. But that doesn't mean you can loan her out to all your friends. Especially without checking with your father and me first."

"That's right," Brooke's stepfather added, looking up from his food. He winked at Brooke. "Don't worry, Brookie. Your show plans are safe—for *this* birthday party, anyway!"

Brooke forced a smile as both her parents chuckled. She was glad that they were taking her side for once. But now she almost wished they wouldn't. It would make her decision a lot easier.

By the time she'd finished helping with the dishes, Brooke had made up her mind to cancel. What was the point of going to the show without Adam? It had all been his idea in the first place anyway. If her parents asked why she wasn't going, she'd just tell them that Foxy was lame—it wasn't as if they'd be able to tell the difference.

She went upstairs and logged on to the Internet, trying to recall the name of the stable where the show was being held. Maybe there was a way to cancel online; if not, at least she could write down the phone number so she could call first thing tomorrow.

When she saw the Pony Post icon on her desktop, she couldn't resist clicking on it before she searched for the farm. She wanted to let her friends know right away what was going on.

There were several new messages since she'd last checked in.

[MADDIE] Brooke! I just saw your note about Foxy bucking. Wowowow! She's such a good girl, I bet you were surprised! No wonder you came off, you were probably too shocked to react, lol! Srsly tho, hope you're feeling OK. And don't be mad at Foxy girl—u know she still luvs u!!!!!

[NINA] Hi again! I was thinking about u during dinner, B. If u ask me (not that u did, lol!) u rly need to stand up to yr parents about the pony ride thing. If it's getting F this upset to have yr lil sibs ride, well, maybe they shouldn't be riding until she's older? Or at least not so often.

[HALEY] Or at least not right before a show. Nina's right, you could talk to your folks again. Maybe that would help?

[NINA] It couldn't hurt, right?

"You don't know my parents," Brooke muttered as she read. Then she blinked, realizing that both Nina and Haley had posted within the past few minutes. She started typing fast.

[BROOKE] Are u guys still here?

The responses came one after the other.

[HALEY] I'm here! Hi B!

[NINA] Me too!

Brooke smiled, instantly feeling less alone. She opened another text box.

> [BROOKE] Doesn't matter much anymore
> about the pony ride thing. B/c I found out
> Adam can't make the show after all. He can't
> even come over tmw and help me practice.
> I was just going to look up the farm website
> to cancel. O well, maybe Foxy & I aren't
> meant to do horse shows just yet. . . .

She posted, then opened a search engine while she waited for her friends to answer. But she'd barely had time to type in her search terms when responses from both her friends popped up.

> [NINA] Are u sure u want to cancel?

> [HALEY] O no, u should totally still go!!! So what if
> A can't come? U and Foxy could still have fun!!!

Brooke was surprised by their reactions. Okay, maybe Haley wouldn't hesitate to go to a show by herself if she had to. She was that serious about her riding. But Nina, too?

[BROOKE] I don't think it's a good idea to go by myself. Esp. after getting bucked off today!!!

Once again her friends' responses came almost immediately.

[HALEY] I'm sure that was a fluke. She's never done it before, right?

[NINA] You and Foxy have a great bond. One bad moment doesn't change that.

[HALEY] Maybe u can just ride over to the show and warm up, see how it goes? If Foxy is too nervous, u can scratch. But if she's being good, u can enter a class or two and take it from there.

[NINA] That's a great idea, H! What do u think, B? Maybe one of yr other friends could go with for moral support, even if they're not into horses?

Brooke appreciated the pep talk, but it wasn't working. Why drag one of her other friends along just to watch her be nervous—and maybe get bucked off again? She was starting to type a response when another post suddenly appeared beneath the others.

[MADDIE] Hey, I'm here too! Are we all rly here at the same time?

[MADDIE] Nvr mind that—B, u don't have to show alone, and u don't even need to bring a non horsey pal! U should get that new girl to come!! What's her name again?

[NINA] Kristin or something, right? Fab idea, Mads!

[HALEY] Ya, she was going to come watch anyway, right? And she sounds super experienced at riding and showing and stuff. Maddie, u r a genius!!!

[MADDIE] I try! So how about it, B?

Brooke chewed her lower lip, thinking about Maddie's suggestion. Could it work? Maybe—but wouldn't it be kind of weird to ask Kiersten to do something like that when they'd really just met?

Besides, bond or not, I don't know if I can forget about that buck between now and Saturday, she thought, her gaze wandering toward the window, even though it was getting too dark to see Foxy out there by now. *I'll just be nervous the whole time, and that won't be good for either of us.*

Her fingers hovered over the keyboard as she tried to figure out how to explain that to her Pony Post friends. They were all so bold and brave in their own ways. She knew they meant well, but this time maybe they just couldn't quite understand how she was feeling.

Noticing her battered copy of *Misty of Chincoteague* lying on the bedside table, she reached over and grabbed it. She'd dreamed of having her own special Chincoteague pony for so long, and up until now Foxy had been everything she could have wished for and more.

If I quit now, will I ever have the nerve to do a show with her? she wondered, running her fingers over the image of Misty. *Or will I be stuck riding in my own backyard forever? Not that there's anything wrong with that. . . .*

She sighed and turned back to the computer, staring at the screen and wondering what she should do.

♦ CHAPTER ♦
11

SATURDAY MORNING DAWNED COLD BUT clear, a perfect late autumn day. Brooke fed Foxy her breakfast as usual and then puttered around the people part of the barn while the mare ate. After a few minutes Brooke went to check on her.

"All done, Foxy?" she murmured, checking the bucket and then burying her fingers in the pony's shaggy chestnut coat. "Betcha want to go out and run around the pasture today, maybe take a nap with the drafts later . . ."

The pony snorted, lifting her head at a sound Brooke couldn't hear. A moment later a smiling face appeared at the half door.

"Hey," Kiersten said breathlessly. "Sorry I'm a little late. I borrowed my brother's mountain bike, and it turns out there's all kinds of gears and stuff on it that I had no idea how to work." She laughed. "I might be able to get a pony over a course of jumps, but I thought I wasn't going to make it down the driveway on that thing!"

Brooke laughed too. "It's okay," she said. "You're not even late; Foxy just finished eating."

"Cool." Kiersten let herself into the pony part of the barn and gave the pony a pat. "Hi again, Foxy. Still as cute as ever, I see!"

Brooke smiled, feeling nervous and excited all at the same time. She still wasn't sure whether she'd made the right decision, but it was too late to change her mind now. Her Pony Post friends had finally convinced her to at least talk to Kiersten about the show. Brooke had gone downstairs to ask her mother for help finding Kiersten's phone number, and when Mrs. Rhodes had heard Kiersten's last name, it turned out she'd sold the Ellises their new house and had their number in her cell.

In fact, she'd whipped out her phone and dialed for

Brooke, which had left Brooke no choice but to call—and Kiersten had said yes right away. She'd even offered to come over on Friday afternoon to meet Foxy and coach Brooke through her final ride before the show.

Now Kiersten was rubbing her hands together as she and Brooke hurried back into the people part of the barn, leaving Foxy to lick the last traces of grain out of her bucket. "Do you have your stuff packed up?" Kiersten asked. "I can carry a bag on the bike. I think."

"I don't have that much." Brooke grabbed the small duffel she'd brought out from the house earlier and dumped the contents of her grooming bucket into it. "Just a few grooming tools and stuff. She'll already have all her tack on, since we're riding over."

"Good point." Kiersten grinned. "So let's get her tacked up and get moving!"

The two of them set to work, grooming Foxy until her shaggy winter coat was as shiny and clean as they could get it, and then saddling her. Brooke mounted, and Kiersten opened the gate to let them out of the pasture. Then she grabbed the sleek silver mountain bike she'd left leaning against the outside wall of the shed.

"Are you sure she's used to riding next to a bike?" Kiersten asked as she swung a leg over the frame. "My old pony would probably think this thing was a horse-eating monster!"

"Definitely." Brooke patted her pony. "We ride with Adam on his bike all the time."

She still felt a twinge of disappointment whenever she thought about Adam. How could he have let her down like this? Sure, she understood how much he'd wanted to be on the basketball team. But couldn't he have told the coach he'd start next week? Or if he couldn't do that, the least he could have done was apologize a little more for leaving her hanging. . . .

With a sigh she did her best to push that all out of her mind. She couldn't afford any negative thoughts today—not if she wanted Foxy to have a good experience at the show. Haley and the others had reminded her of that last night.

"Come on, let's go," she told Kiersten. "It's this way."

The show barn was just a half hour ride across several

farm fields and through a couple of patches of woods. As they crossed the last field, they started to be able to hear the commotion of the show. Foxy pricked her ears, slowing her pace a little as a loudspeaker crackled.

Kiersten glanced over, huffing and puffing after her bike ride. "She okay?"

"I think so." Brooke patted the pony. "Come on, Foxy. You're fine."

But the mare seemed to grow taller and more animated with every step after that. They had to cross a quiet country road to reach the stable's property, and Foxy spooked at the sound of her own hoof on the asphalt.

"She's definitely on her toes," Kiersten said once they'd made it across safely. "That's no surprise, since you said she hasn't been to a show since summer."

"Yeah." Brooke squeezed her legs against the mare's side as Foxy skittered sideways at a blowing leaf. "And that one was at the same place where she'd been for two weeks already."

"It'll be okay." Kiersten got off and started wheeling the bike up the stable drive, eyeing the busy stable grounds ahead of them as she walked. "Most horses settle down after a few minutes. And Foxy seems supersensible."

"She is." Brooke gulped as Foxy spooked again, this time at the sound of a car horn somewhere farther down the road. "Usually."

She was tempted to get off and lead Foxy instead of riding her. But Kiersten was acting as if Foxy's behavior was no big deal, and Brooke didn't want to look like a chicken in front of her new friend. So she gritted her teeth and did her best to stay calm.

Foxy just needs me to be confident, she told herself, remembering how different the pony had been when Adam had ridden her the other day, even though he wasn't even a particularly experienced rider. *I'm sure she'll settle down soon, like Kiersten said.*

They made their way past the farm's big stone house to the show grounds beyond. The place was pretty small, with just a rustic wooden barn, a large outdoor ring, and several roomy pastures. One of the pastures had been given over to parking, and at least a dozen horse trailers were already in there, along with plenty of cars. Horses and riders were milling around in the parking area and in the crushed stone courtyard between the barn and the ring. Spectators had already set up lawn chairs along the long sides of the ring, where a course of colorful crossrails was set up, decorated with fake flowers and pots of greens. A sign on the gate read SHOW RING—NO SCHOOLING.

"Looks like they only have the one ring." Kiersten glanced around. "I wonder where— Oh, wait, okay, I see the schooling ring."

She pointed to a large paddock near the barn. The gate was propped open with a cinder block, and half a dozen riders were in there trotting around or jumping their horses and ponies over the crossrail and simple vertical someone had set up in the center. On the fence, a sign read SCHOOLING RING.

"So we warm up in there?" Brooke halted Foxy at the edge of the show grounds. The pony's head was up, and she let out a snort and then a loud whinny. Somewhere in the parking area, another horse whinnied back.

Kiersten smiled and patted the pony on the neck. "It's

okay, Foxy girl." She glanced up at Brooke. "Why don't you ride her around and let her relax and get a look at everything? I can go get your number and sign you up for the stuff we talked about."

After finishing their schooling the evening before, the two of them had pored over the show's schedule on Brooke's laptop. They'd chosen a couple of divisions that looked suitable—the first was a beginner horse class for green horses and ponies, and the other was an equitation division for riders who were new to showing. Brooke hadn't been able to miss the fact that those were the same two divisions that Adam had mentioned when he'd first told her about the show, though she was trying not to think about him today.

"Um, okay." Brooke was glad that Kiersten was there to help. She hadn't even known that she needed to get a number, though she could see that many of the other riders already had cardboard cards tied around their waists, with big black numerals on them.

Kiersten wheeled her bike off toward the sign-in table over by the barn, soon disappearing into the crowd. Brooke glanced briefly at the schooling ring, then turned Foxy in the opposite direction and rode her toward the edge of the parking area, where it was quieter.

Twenty minutes later Kiersten spotted them riding circles at the walk and hurried over. "Hey, there you are!" she said with a smile, holding up a piece of cardboard with a string flopping from it. "Here's your number."

"Thanks." Brooke dismounted and took it from her, handing over Foxy's reins in exchange. Then she tied the number around her waist like she'd seen the other riders do, so it was centered on her lower back.

Kiersten took a few steps toward the rings, Foxy trailing along behind her, and peered at the schooling paddock. "Your first division starts pretty soon," she said. "You should probably take Foxy in and warm up over that crossrail a couple of times."

Brooke swallowed hard as she followed her friend's gaze. Even more riders had crowded into the schooling ring by then, and all of them seemed to be going in different directions at different gaits.

Kiersten hadn't waited for an answer and was leading

the pony off toward the gate. Brooke followed, trying to tell herself that she'd be fine.

Things looked even more chaotic from right next to the ring. Brooke took a few deep breaths, then checked her helmet strap to make sure it was buckled tightly.

"Okay, up you go," Kiersten said cheerfully, looping Foxy's reins back over her head and then holding the bridle to keep the pony steady.

After touching her helmet strap one last time, Brooke stuck her left foot into the stirrup and swung aboard. Foxy had started to feel calmer out in the relative quiet of the parking area, but now she felt tense and on edge again as she stared at the horses and ponies rushing around in the schooling ring.

"Good luck, and be careful." Kiersten smiled, checked to make sure Foxy's girth was tight, and then patted the pony on the shoulder. "Looks a little crazy in there. As usual for a schooling ring!"

Brooke nodded and glanced toward the main ring. It looked so nice and peaceful out there; she wished she could just go straight in without dealing with the schooling ring.

But Kiersten hadn't suggested that, so Brooke guessed it wasn't how things were done.

She gave Foxy a nudge with her heels, steering her toward the open gate. A wildly spotted Appaloosa came charging out at a trot right before they got there, and Foxy froze and snorted as the horse rushed past.

"Someone come wipe off my boots!" the Appaloosa's rider hollered, barely seeming to notice that she'd almost crashed into Brooke.

"It's okay, girl," Brooke whispered, taking a few deep breaths and trying to remember what Nina had told her about how to calm herself down. But she couldn't recall what Nina had said to do, so Brooke just gulped in one more breath and then nudged her pony forward again.

This time they made it through the gate and into the ring. The crossrail in the center looked a million miles away, with horses and ponies of all shapes and sizes passing between here and there. Training her gaze on it, Brooke urged Foxy forward.

At that moment a tall bay horse cantered past less than

an arm's length in front of them. Foxy snorted and tossed her head, wheeling sideways.

Brooke froze, flashing back to the seconds before that buck the other day. Her hands clenched tightly on the reins, pulling back so hard that Foxy shook her head and backed up.

"Hey!" an annoyed voice yelled from right behind them.

Glancing over her shoulder, Brooke saw that Foxy had almost crashed into a stout dapple gray pony walking along the rail. Oops!

"S-sorry," Brooke called, though the other pony had already trotted away. Foxy started turning around again, letting out a panicky snort, and Brooke just sat there, unable to react and wondering what her parents would think if her pony came galloping home without her. . . .

A second later Kiersten materialized at Foxy's head, taking the reins and talking soothingly to the pony. She led them back to the gate and paused just inside.

"You okay?" she asked, squinting up at Brooke.

Brooke just shook her head, suddenly on the verge of

tears. Realizing she was still clutching the reins, she let them go entirely, leaving Kiersten to hold her pony still.

Kiersten bit her lip, then glanced through the gate. "Coming out!" she hollered, leading Foxy out of the ring.

Once they were a safe distance outside, Brooke managed to control her trembling limbs long enough to dismount. She sank to the ground against a fence post and closed her eyes.

Kiersten pulled the reins over Foxy's head and let her lower her head to graze on the weeds beneath the fence line. Then she squatted in front of Brooke.

"Hey," she said softly. "What's the matter?"

Brooke looked up at her, a couple of tears squeezing out, despite her best efforts to stop them. The shaking had subsided a little, but her heart was still racing.

"I can't do this," she blurted out. "I'm sorry."

The other girl's eyes widened in surprise. "What do you mean?"

"The show." Brooke took a deep breath. "I thought it'd be okay, but it's not. I can't do it."

She felt horrible. Why did she have to be such a

chicken? She'd let her pony down and humiliated herself, and now she looked like an idiot in front of Kiersten, who'd probably never want to talk to her again.

And what about the Pony Posters? she thought miserably. *They're all going to think I'm a big loser. I'm sure none of them would flake out like this.*

She grimaced, trying to imagine what she was going to tell them—bold Haley, confident Maddie, cool-as-a-cucumber Nina. What would they say to her if they were here right now?

She forgot about that as Kiersten grabbed her hand and squeezed it.

"Listen, this is just show nerves again," she said. "You can do this! You and Foxy are a great team, remember?"

"Maybe at home we are." Brooke sighed and picked at a blade of brownish grass beside her. "But I'm thinking we just aren't cut out for showing."

"Sure you are," Kiersten urged. "You did so great yesterday, and—"

"No." Brooke cut her off. "Um, thanks for the pep talk, but there's no point. I can't ride in the show. I just can't."

Kiersten didn't say anything for a second. She stood up and looked over at the rings, then at Foxy. Finally she turned back toward Brooke.

"I have an idea," she said. "Would it be okay— I mean, do you think maybe *I* should ride Foxy in the first division?"

Surprised, Brooke glanced up at her. "Huh?"

"Listen, you already offered to let me ride Foxy anytime, right? So I promise I'm not just being pushy." Kiersten grinned, talking very fast now. "But the thing is, you worked so hard to get here, and I know Foxy can do it." She paused and shrugged. "I'm just not sure *you* know that. Know what I mean?"

Brooke stared at her, trying to take in what she was saying. "But the way she bucked—and she's still green, and, well . . ."

"If you say no, that's fine." Kiersten shrugged. "But I'm pretty sure I can handle her."

Brooke thought about that. Everything Kiersten had ever said made her sound like a pretty experienced rider.

What's the worst that could happen? Brooke thought.

All sorts of answers to that question immediately

started dancing around in her head. After all, Brooke had never actually seen Kiersten ride. What if she talked a good game but actually rode more like Brooke's little brother, hauling Foxy around by the reins? What if Foxy bucked her off, or wouldn't stop spooking? Brooke had worked so hard on the pony's training, and she'd hate to see it ruined. . . .

Kiersten was watching her, waiting. "At least let me take her back into the warm-up ring," she suggested. "You don't want to let her remember a bad experience in there, right? Then you can decide about the division."

"I just don't know," Brooke said slowly. "I mean, I appreciate the offer, but I don't want anything bad to happen."

"I know. But listen. Foxy is a great pony. She has a super-sweet temperament and good basic training. All she needs is . . ." Kiersten paused and shot Brooke a sidelong look.

Brooke blinked, suddenly thinking back again to Adam taking Foxy over those new jumps recently. "A confident ride?" Brooke said softly.

The other girl grinned sheepishly. "No offense. I just

think maybe you're too nervous to, you know, deal with a pony who's a little nervous too."

"Yeah." Brooke thought about that. "Maybe you're right."

"So maybe all you need is to see her go with someone else," Kiersten went on, tugging on the reins as the pony tried to wander off in search of a tastier grazing spot. "Who knows? Maybe that'll be all you need to be ready to ride her in that eq division later!"

Brooke didn't know about that. But suddenly she was tired of worrying. Besides, Kiersten was right. A pony was always learning, for better or for worse. So if Brooke couldn't give Foxy a good show experience herself, maybe Kiersten could. And if not? Well, Brooke would have to worry about that later.

"Okay," she said quickly, not wanting to give herself time for second-guessing. She pulled off her helmet and handed it to Kiersten. "Let's try it."

◆ CHAPTER ◆

12

KIERSTEN SMILED. "GOOD. COME ON, FOXY—
we don't have much time."

Soon the stirrups were adjusted and she was in the
saddle. Brooke stayed at the pony's head as they walked
back over to the schooling ring, her hand hovering near
the bridle, ready to grab the reins if Foxy did anything
silly.

To her surprise, though, the mare seemed fine. Yes,
her ears were still pricked and her head was a little high.
But Kiersten steered Foxy easily past a crying toddler and
a couple of prancey horses, without Foxy doing anything
more than pricking her ears and swishing her tail.

"Good luck." Brooke stepped aside as Foxy reached the gate and halted.

Kiersten shot her a quick smile. "Thanks." Then she rode into the ring, turning Foxy immediately to the left to follow a big chestnut horse trotting along at the rail.

Brooke stood at the fence, clutching the top board so hard that her fingernails dug into the wood as she watched them warm up. Foxy still looked more alert than usual, and once she skittered to the side when a speedy little pony passed by a little too closely. But none of it seemed to faze Kiersten, who looked as relaxed as if she were just ambling along out in Foxy's quiet pasture at home. After trotting and cantering in each direction, Kiersten aimed the pony at the crossrail in the middle of the ring.

"Heads up! Crossrail!" she shouted.

Another pony that had been coming at the jump from the opposite direction veered off, and Foxy cantered up to the jump and leaped over it, leaving so much room to spare that Brooke was surprised that Kiersten didn't get bounced right out of the saddle. But she just laughed and patted Foxy, then turned to take the jump again in the other direction. This time Foxy jumped more normally, and after two more times Kiersten patted her once more and then rode out of the ring.

"Wow," Brooke said when the pair halted beside her. "That looked great! You're a really good rider. And Foxy really seems to like you."

Kiersten smiled. "Thanks. I like her, too. Her trot is amazingly smooth!" She rubbed the pony's withers and shot Brooke a sidelong smile. "So what do you think? Can we give that beginner horse division a try?"

Brooke smiled back. "Absolutely!"

A few minutes later Brooke stood at the fence watching as Kiersten steered Foxy over the course of crossrails in the main ring. Foxy looked a little anxious on their opening circle, and she hesitated slightly in front of the first jump, which was decorated with pots of bright red plastic roses on each end.

But Kiersten urged her forward, and a second later the pony was arcing over the fence and cantering off toward the next one. Brooke held her breath through the first half of the course, but let it out when she realized that her pony was doing great. She got a little nervous again when the flat class started, since that involved all the horses and ponies in the division walking, trotting, and cantering in the ring at the same time. But Kiersten managed to keep Foxy mostly away from the others, and aside from a little spook when a spectator cheered right next to her, the pony once again performed like she'd been showing for ages.

In the end Foxy came in third in the entire division and even earned a "nice pony" from the judge when she handed over the ribbons. Brooke was bursting with pride as she borrowed Kiersten's cell phone to snap a few pictures of Foxy posing with her yellow ribbon flapping from her bridle.

When Brooke turned around to return the phone, she spotted several familiar figures heading their way from the direction of the parking lot.

"There you are, sweetie!" Brooke's mother hurried forward, looking casual and sporty in a pair of spotless jeans, black leather ankle boots, and an argyle sweater that Brooke guessed she probably thought looked horsey. "Surprise!"

Brooke's stepfather was right behind her, holding one of the twins' hands in each of his. "The birthday party finished a little early, so we thought we'd come cheer you on."

"Yeah," Ethan spoke up. "Owen threw up all over the cake!"

Emma giggled. "It was gross!"

Brooke barely heard them. She was amazed to see Adam right behind the others. "Hey," he said, coming over to pat Foxy. "Practice got postponed."

Just then Brooke's mother noticed the ribbon flapping from Foxy's bridle. "Oh dear. Did we miss everything?" she exclaimed. "But it looks like you and Foxy did well—congrats, Brooke!"

"Thanks." Brooke blushed. "But it wasn't me. Kiersten rode her in the classes."

"Yeah, Brooke was nice enough to give me the first turn," Kiersten spoke up. "But she's going to ride in the next division. Right, Brooke?"

Brooke took a deep breath, looking from her new friend to the others. "Maybe," she said. Then she looked at Foxy, and her heart swelled with love and pride. How could she ever have doubted that Foxy could do this? "I mean, yes. For sure."

She felt a shiver of nerves—but some excitement, too. After seeing how well Foxy had done with Kiersten, Brooke realized she couldn't wait to give it a try herself!

The equitation division didn't go quite as smoothly as the first one. In the flat class Brooke accidentally asked her pony to canter once when she was supposed to be trotting, and in her first jump course one of Foxy's hooves clunked a rail and sent it clattering to the ground, which spooked Foxy and made Brooke have to circle before the next jump. Still, when it was all over, they ended up finishing in sixth place on the flat and fourth in their second over-fences class.

"Yay, Brooke!" Ethan cheered as Kiersten hung the two new ribbons on the pony's bridle. "And yay, Foxy!"

"Yeah," Emma added with a giggle. "She's a cow pony *and* a jumping pony!"

That gave Brooke an idea. She glanced at her parents. "They're doing some fun classes after the main divisions are done," she told them. "Including a Western leadline class for kids. Maybe I could take E in that one if he wants?"

"Really?" Ethan shouted. "Hooray!"

"What about me?" Emma whined.

Brooke tugged on her sister's pigtail. "Maybe you could do the English leadline class."

"Oh." Emma thought about that for a second. "Okay! I'd rather be a jumper than a cowgirl anyway."

Brooke laughed, not bothering to explain that there wouldn't be any jumping. Meanwhile her stepfather pulled out his car keys. "I'll run home and grab your Western saddle," he offered, hurrying off.

"Thanks," Brooke's mother called after him. Then she patted Emma on the head. "Come on, everyone. Let's go get a snack to celebrate, hmm?" She smiled at Kiersten, who was holding Foxy's reins. "Maybe we can even find some cookies for Foxy."

As the others wandered toward the refreshment stand, Adam pulled Brooke aside. "Hey," he said. "Um, sorry about bailing on you."

"That's okay," Brooke said, even though it wasn't, not

really. But what was the point of making him feel bad, especially when everything had turned out so great in the end?

"Cool." He looked relieved. "Anyway, that Kiersten girl seems nice."

"Yeah, she is." Brooke shot a look at Kiersten, who was laughing over something Emma had just said. "Really nice."

Brooke was pretty sure the two of them were going to be good friends. It would be fun to have someone to share her pony with—well, other than the twins. Maybe her siblings would want to keep riding, and maybe not. Either way, Brooke was sure now that she and Foxy could handle it—with a little help from her new friend.

That evening after dinner Brooke was so exhausted, she could barely drag herself over to the counter to put her dishes into the sink. She picked up a dishtowel, but her mother immediately plucked it out of her hand.

"Your father can dry tonight, sweetie," she said, tossing the towel at Brooke's stepfather. "You go on up to bed. You've had a long day."

Brooke thanked her and headed upstairs. After peeling off her show clothes, she stumbled into the bathroom and took a quick shower, not wanting to go to bed covered in dust and sweat and horse hair.

The water and the sweet smell of her favorite raspberry shampoo actually woke her up a little. So after pulling on her pajamas, she grabbed her laptop and sat cross-legged on her bed, not wanting to leave the Pony Post in suspense about how the show had gone.

First she uploaded some of the photos her stepfather, Kiersten, and Adam had forwarded from their phones. Then she opened a text box and filled the Pony Posters in on everything that had happened at the show, from her attack of nerves in the schooling ring to Kiersten's great ride in the beginner horse division to her own performance in the equitation classes. And of course she couldn't forget to mention her little brother's triumphant, blue-ribbon-winning ride in the leadline class. Okay, so all the kids had won a blue ribbon, but that hadn't stopped Ethan from declaring himself the world's greatest cowboy ever!

Finally she was pretty sure she'd told them everything. Reading back over what she'd just posted, though, she realized there was one more thing she wanted to say.

[BROOKE] By the way, I almost forgot to thank u guys for talking me into doing the show even tho I was scared. And also for always believing in me and Foxy, even when I wasn't quite sure I believed in us myself. The good news is, I def believe in us now! And the next time I get nervous—and I know there will be a next time, lol!—I can look back on this day and know that Foxy and I can do anything!!!

◆ Glossary ◆

bronc riders: Riders who take part in bronc riding, a rodeo event in which competitors try to stay on the back of a bucking horse.

bucking: When a horse lowers its head and kicks out or up with both hind legs. This movement is harmless horseplay when performed at liberty in the pasture but can unseat a rider when performed under saddle.

paddock: A fenced enclosure for horses. In the US the term "paddock" is usually used for a relatively small enclosure (as opposed to pasture for a larger one), while in some other parts of the world "paddock" can refer to an enclosure of any size.

circles and figure eights: Riders often practice different figures to work on steering, bending, and other elements of proper riding. Circles and figure eights are two popular exercises.

cow pony: A term for a cowboy's horse, especially one used for herding cattle.

equitation classes: In English hunter jumper shows (and some other disciplines), an equitation class is judged solely on the rider's performance and abilities, as opposed to most other classes, in which the horse or overall performance is judged.

jockey: The person who rides a horse in a race.

mustangs: Feral horses who live wild in the American West. They are thought to be descended from horses brought to the continent by Spanish settlers. Some mustangs are rounded up, tamed, and trained as riding horses.

schooling ring: As used in this book, the schooling ring—also called a warm-up ring—is a riding ring at a show that isn't used for showing but rather for warming up, cooling down, or schooling before or after show classes.

two-point position: This is when a rider lifts his or her seat out of the saddle, balancing on only two points of contact—his or her two feet in the stirrups. It's also sometimes called "jumping position" or "half seat."

Marguerite Henry's Ponies of Chincoteague is inspired by the award-winning books by Marguerite Henry, the beloved author of such classic horse stories as *King of the Wind*; *Misty of Chincoteague*; *Justin Morgan Had a Horse*; *Stormy, Misty's Foal*; *Misty's Twilight*; and *Album of Horses*, among many other titles.

Learn more about the world of Marguerite Henry at www.MistyofChincoteague.org.

Don't miss the
next book in the series!

Book 7: *Back in the Saddle*

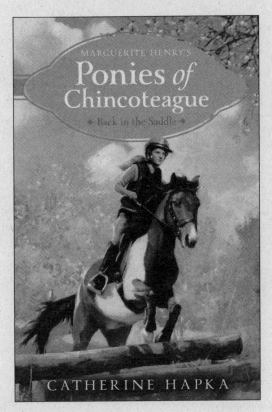

Saddle up for a new world of classic horse tales!

For a full round-up of pony stories inspired by Marguerite Henry's *Misty of Chincoteague* visit **PoniesOfChincoteague.com**!